SAINTS & MARTYRS

Martin Penny

Saints & Martyrs

THE FIRST
ALLISON COUSINS
INVESTIGATION

BLACK SPRING **CRIME SERIES**

First published in 2020
by Black Spring Press
An imprint of the Black Spring Press Group (Eyewear Publishing Ltd)

Suite 333, 19-21 Crawford Street
Marylebone, London W1H 1PJ
United Kingdom

Cover design and typeset by Edwin Smet
Cover image by Getty Images

All rights reserved
© 2020 Martin Penny

The right of Martin Penny to be identified as author of
this work has been asserted in accordance with section 77
of the Copyright, Designs and Patents Act 1988

ISBN 978-1-912477-98-2

For my parents
whose continued support
made it possible – and for never
giving up hope of seeing
it in print
&
My wonderful wife and children
without whom it wouldn't
mean anything

Martin Penny was born in London and currently lives in Turkey with his wife and two children. After an early flirtation with accounting, he found his true vocation managing a second hand bookshop. He retired in 2015. He is now working on future instalments of *The Allison Cousins Investigations*, which will continue with *Death & The Angel*.

London, November 1994
Paddington Green High Security
Police Station

'Start at the beginning.'

I stared straight ahead, struggling to retain my composure. I tried hard not to acknowledge my interrogator, but my impassive façade was already in danger of crumbling in response to his opening gambit. Despite my best efforts, a sigh escaped my lungs. My hands rested heavily in my lap. I could feel them trembling through the blood-splattered fabric of my jeans. He hadn't even allowed me to wash. Forensics needed to analyse the dried blood and gunshot residue. Maybe I looked better than I felt.

He faced me across a scarred wooden table whose surface bore the marks of decades of interviews. Chief Superintendent Jeffries was a senior officer frequently employed investigating his colleagues' alleged transgressions. His enquiries were notoriously thorough, and the merest indication of impropriety normally resulted in summary dismissal. He was well into his fifties and his pockmarked face was framed with grey: not just the hair, but the unnatural pallor of his skin. His eyes were unnaturally close together and appeared to balance on the tip of his long, straight nose. I knew from experience that he was short of patience and now I, through no fault of my own, found myself in his sights.

I'd had a three hour car journey to prepare my story, during which I'd thrashed it around so many times in my head that I was having difficulty keeping track of all the incidents that had taken place. I was striving to remember the sequence of the sometimes fictitious tale I was attempting to fashion. If I wasn't careful, I'd trip myself up and be forced to resort to the truth. Not a good career move: not for me, and certainly not for Jordan.

I couldn't understand the indecent haste to proceedings. In fact, the whole situation was seriously disturbing. Strictly speaking, in accordance with current police procedures, my clothes should have been bagged for analysis and I should have been provided with a paper jumpsuit. Additionally, I should have had a solicitor or Federation Rep sitting beside me and there was no way that Jeffries should be interviewing me alone. I knew he was a stickler for rules and regulations. There had to be a very good reason why he was ignoring so many elements of PACE. I had my suspicions but they wouldn't be confirmed until much later.

Before recounting the events of the previous three weeks, I should explain that I'm a serving police constable: WPC Allison Cousins. At least I think I still am, hanging on by my fingertips. If anyone learned the real story, I'd be down the job centre quicker than a greyhound on acid. Relatively new to the force, I'm still in my probation period and struggling to come to terms with life on the street. I'm not big or strong, neither am I overly imbued with self-confidence. Fortunately, my colleague Jordan Lassiter had enough of those qualities for both of us.

I'll admit to being 5'6' on a good day, as long as I'm not standing in totally flat shoes. There isn't a lot of me and despite eating too much junk food, I can't put on weight. My appearance isn't anything to write home about, and I'm constantly being told that I have a whiny, irritating voice. I put it down to the fact that my father is from Wisconsin and somewhere along the line I must have inherited a slight transatlantic drawl. I keep my hair pretty short. It's thick, straight and completely unmanageable. In my youth, I took great pride in growing it until it reached my waist, forever hooking it behind my ears in an attempt to see where I was going. Now my ears stick out. I make a point of excusing myself whenever the family photo albums come out.

'When you're ready,' the unsympathetic Jeffries reminded me. His sunken eyes looked bored and disinterested, but I knew he was ready to pounce on any inconsistency in my responses. The tapes whirred on their spools, capturing white noise while I thought about what to say.

I'd encountered Chief Superintendent Jeffries several times during the course of events. Each time he'd treated me with nothing more than idle curiosity, like a fly caught in Jordan's ever-expanding web. I'd been no more than a tacky piece of window dressing, a bauble hanging from her Christmas tree. Now he believed he could get to Jordan through me. I was equally determined to ensure that he didn't.

The thought of Jordan brought a fleeting smile to my lips. I made certain it didn't travel any further. My last memory of her ensured it didn't complete the journey across the rest of my face. She was a Detective Sergeant on a neighbouring police force and I didn't know whether she was alive or dead. When I'd last seen her in the early hours of the morning, paramedics had successfully scraped what was left of her off the floor and eased it onto a stretcher. She'd lost a lot of blood. Her right leg was a mess and she was in and out of consciousness. Despite her robust constitution, I figured she was tottering on the verge. I hadn't realised how attached to her I'd become, and the thought of her fighting for her life moistened my eyes.

'Start from the reconstruction,' Jeffries suggested, growing weary of the silence.

I shuddered: it hadn't been one of my finest hours.

'How's Jordan?' I asked.

He shook his head and replied stoically, 'I don't have any news.'

When I first met Jordan, she was already suspended. It wasn't an entirely unknown situation for her and she tried not to let it interfere with her regular day-to-day schedule. She was a shadowy figure at the best of times, frequently the subject of whispered conversations but rarely seen. Her exploits were the stuff of hushed canteen gossip and her methods had landed her in a series of confrontations with her senior officers.

She still had some friends in high places, and to keep her out of trouble she'd been recruited to a team that provided protection for visiting heads of state. Her job was to liaise with visiting security teams and stay one step ahead of the terrorists. As such, she was one of the few highly trained officers licensed to carry a firearm. She regarded the task as a chore, only endured because it left her free to become involved in whatever she wanted, within reason. But it was her reason that was frequently called into question. Her one guiding light was the apprehension of criminals, and (it was whispered) she wasn't too choosy how she went about it. Her arrest record alone should have made her fireproof. In addition, she'd received three commendations and a medal for bravery. She wasn't over-impressed: 'They either had to give me a medal or sack me,' she'd told me. I later learned it was true.

'When did you first meet Jordan Lassiter?' Jeffries asked, trying a different approach.

Of course, that was what he was really interested in. The fact that without much help from anyone else on the force, the two of us had tracked down a serial killer, was immaterial. Lawrence Arnold had been responsible for the death of an as yet unconfirmed number of young people, but what he really wanted was to hang Jordan out to dry.

'Is Arnold dead?' I asked. I needed to be certain.

He shook his head again. 'I don't have any news.'

When did I first meet Jordan? It had only been twenty-three days ago, but it felt like a lifetime. It was just after the reconstruction. I knew I should never have become involved.

I'd only just returned from it when I was summoned for a debriefing. Tentatively, I'd knocked on Sergeant Ramsden's door, hoping he wasn't there.

'Come in,' I heard.

I sighed and strode in, attempting to portray a degree of confidence I didn't feel. I shut the door firmly behind me and took the offered seat. I'd had a shower in the locker room and changed out of the clothes I'd been wearing, donning my black all-purpose police sweater. I hoped there was no lingering smell of vomit, but I wasn't surprised when Ramsden went straight to the window and opened it.

'How do you feel?' Ramsden asked without any emotion. The central ceiling light reflected brightly on his bald head and highlighted the tufts of dark hair around his ears. I tried to remember that I'd always thought of him as kind. He had bright, gentle eyes and a soft, rounded mouth. Besides, he'd never had a bad word to say about me, yet.

'Fine,' I replied hesitantly.

He didn't appear convinced. 'So, what happened?'

'Must have been something I ate,' I told him, but we both knew it wasn't true.

He shook his head. 'What were your impressions?' he went on. 'Anything you picked up on the street? You *were* the centre of attention. Maybe you noticed something.'

'I didn't feel anything at all,' I stated quietly. 'Not until we got close to the pub.'

'What did you feel then?'

I thought for a few moments. 'Claustrophobic: I thought I was being watched. Not like before, when everyone was looking at me. I felt like someone was watching, staring.' I held my hands out in futility. How could I explain it when I didn't understand it myself? It *was* a kind of claustrophobia; everything closed in on me and suddenly I was having trouble breathing. There was a distinct whiff of malice in the air. No! The smell was something I recognized. I just couldn't put my finger on it. Then again, it might have been the bacon sandwich I'd had for breakfast.

'You almost passed out,' he reminded me.

I had the decency to look embarrassed. 'I felt dizzy.'

He nodded sympathetically. 'I appreciate your help. I know you didn't want to do it and I know I twisted your arm.' If he was expecting any argument he was disappointed. So far it was all true. 'I just wanted to thank you personally.'

I nodded, unused to gratitude.

'Sometimes duty calls in a difficult way,' he continued.

We'd already endured a lengthy silence when we heard a commotion outside. Ramsden's eyebrows rose and he was momentarily distracted. The source of the disturbance was drawing closer. We both turned and looked at the closed door. Ramsden was staring open-mouthed when it burst open.

Startled, I turned in my seat to face the figure striding confidently into the room. She was big, and she was angry! Involuntarily, I shrank back in my chair and tried to appear as small and unthreatening as possible. I stared straight ahead. The maze of cracks in the plaster on the opposite wall was interesting. I thought the middle section had an uncanny resemblance to a map of Central African states.

The towering figure ignored me and approached Ramsden's desk. 'We need to talk,' she told him abruptly.

'Jordan! I'm in a meeting, for Christ's sake!'

Jordan Lassiter! That explained everything. Her physique was nearly as well renowned as her lack of humour. She was in her mid-twenties and weighed about fourteen stone without an ounce of fat. Like other muscle-bound fanatics dedicated to perfecting their body, her bust had virtually disappeared and the impressions her perpetually taut muscles made through her thin clothing were highly impressive. However, I couldn't help noticing how the simplicity of her outfit, a white T-shirt and blue jeans topped by a stylish black wool jacket, afforded her a surprising elegance. Her white trainers were new and looked expensive. Her legs seemed to extend as high as my chest and her long blond hair was parted in the middle and tied back severely. In anything other than bright light she could have been mistaken for a man with a ponytail. Her face was sharply contoured and appeared incapable of a simple smile, but there was something in those eyes. Something disturbing...

Unperturbed, she stared at Ramsden for an unnerving

period of time, before hissing, 'You're drinking again.'

He took a deep breath. 'Jordan...'

For the first time, she registered me. I was cowering silently in my chair, making certain I didn't make eye contact. 'Leave,' she told me quietly.

'Jordan!' cried Ramsden, exasperated. Then, with a long sigh, 'Allison, this is Jordan Lassiter. Jordan, Allison Cousins.' I seriously considered saying something, but quickly thought better of it. I did manage a curt nod in her direction, while conscious of those eyes boring into me. 'Sorry,' Ramsden said. 'Can you give us a few minutes?'

Just for a second I was confused, my eyes darting between the two of them. Then I made the mistake of establishing eye contact with Jordan. I didn't hang about. I grabbed my bag and fled to the sanctuary of the outer office.

I waited impatiently, perched on the end of a desk, trying not to listen to the raised voices muffled by the stout wooden door. A few minutes later, the door opened and a red-faced Jordan Lassiter filled its frame. I thought she looked furious, but on reflection decided that that must have been her natural expression. She held the door and with a curt flick of her head indicated that I could enter. When I was within touching distance, our eyes met again. I struggled to break contact as I stared up into those huge green eyes. It felt like she was probing me for any sign of weakness.

In the doorway as I squeezed past, Jordan whispered, 'You smell of vomit.'

I looked back at her and thought I could detect a trace of a grin.

'She's on our side, Jordan!' Ramsden called after her as she disappeared down the corridor without a backward glance.

I resumed my seat, feeling as though Jordan had stripped me of any pretence and exposed the bare bones of my inadequate personality. 'That was Jordan Lassiter?' I asked rather unnecessarily.

A girl named Celia Potter was missing. The police were sufficiently anxious to stage a time consuming and expensive reconstruction of her last known walk to work. They hoped it might jog the memories of anyone who'd seen her that night, maybe talking to someone. A decent description could possibly lead directly to discovering her location. Nobody was certain whether a crime had taken place, so her status was classified as low, but she'd been missing ten days and her family was desperate. She'd simply vanished.

Understandably, Celia's disappearance wasn't exactly the stuff to excite Jordan. She had her sights set on something far more enticing: a Chinese diplomat who was indulging in illicit trysts with pre-pubescent schoolgirls. Somehow, and I didn't want to know the full details, she'd got her hands on four CDs full of the resulting photos: enough proof to put him behind bars for years. Only he had diplomatic immunity.

This situation led to the incident that had resulted in her latest suspension. Jordan had 'acquired' the disks but was frustrated to find them password protected. She had the evidence in her hands but couldn't use it. Although she *thought* she knew what she had, once she'd broken the encryption, they might have turned out to be Wagner's *Flight of the Valkyries*. Acting on her own initiative, naturally, she'd confronted him and 'during the ensuing struggle' her weapon had been discharged. The man wasn't badly hurt, but as Ramsden later told me, 'He wouldn't be having any more children.' Jordan was a very good shot.

Entirely coincidentally, during the course of the confrontation Jordan discovered the password. Her statement made clear that the two events were entirely unconnected. I knew better. It was a case of Jordan extracting her version of justice. When the Chinese got wind of the unpleasant smell in the air, they packed the offender on the first plane back to Beijing. He had immunity. The law in this country couldn't touch him, but I fancied he'd remember his encounter with one of its more unpredictable officers.

Chapter 2

'Why don't you just start at the beginning?' Jeffries demanded. We were sitting in a simple interview room, just the two of us. It felt odd. I was more accustomed to sitting on the other side of the table. Normally interviews were not conducted alone, but they didn't seem to think I posed much of a threat. Neither had Lawrence Arnold. It was that mistake that probably cost him his life.

I started to talk and the spinning tapes recorded my words for posterity. They would probably play them to future generations of cadets: 'This is a perfect illustration of how *not* to go about a police investigation.'

I told him all about the reconstruction. For some reason, Sergeant Ramsden thought that something dreadful had happened to Celia Potter. After producing the 'Missing' posters, he started talking about a reconstruction. I remember my heart dropped as I saw one of his posters on a notice board. Celia Potter bore a striking resemblance to someone I encountered every morning in my bathroom mirror. It didn't take long to work out who'd be volunteered to play the part of the missing girl.

The description on the poster claimed Celia was 5'7', but she was probably vain enough to lie about it. Like me, she wasn't attractive in a regular way. Her eyebrows were wild and untamed, her nose was crooked and her mouth too narrow. Apart from that, I suppose she was okay. In the picture, her strawberry blonde hair was fashioned into an unkempt bob. She had nice eyes. Everyone has to have at least one redeeming feature.

A WPC had been dispatched to the nearest discount store and selected an assortment of clothes that almost coincided with the grainy black and white CCTV pictures of her walking towards the pub. It was understandably difficult selecting colours, but eventually, everything appeared plausible. As luck would have it, the best matches of colour and style had only been available in a limited range of sizes.

So it was that I trudged miserably along the High Street in clothes and shoes that nearly matched Celia's. Everything was a size too small. I could hardly breathe in the skin-tight sweater with which I'd been provided. It was a miserable afternoon and rain gusted into my eyes. And all the while I tried not to think of the girl in whose footsteps I was treading.

Video cameras recorded the scene and the tape was made available for local news broadcasts. Further copies of the poster were distributed to anyone passing and uniformed constables questioned pedestrians.

At that point we didn't know what had become of Celia, but as I neared the end of the street, approaching the pub at which she would have worked had she reached there, I felt something. You know how it feels when you're sure someone is watching you? It's an uneasy feeling, and I scoured the grubby windowpanes of the upper storeys trying to locate its source. I'd become accustomed to being the centre of attention. I was after all the star of this tragic pantomime, but this was different. I got the definite impression that someone was watching me, someone who knew all about Celia and what had become of her.

Yes, it was irrational. What can I say?

The feeling was so strong that I became increasingly disorientated and nearly passed out. My nostrils were full of a familiar, yet unidentifiable smell. My legs lost their rigidity and suddenly my bacon sandwich and cup of tea made an unwelcome reappearance down the front of my sweater. A PC caught me before I fell over, boldly risking damage to his crisp clean uniform. Maybe it was just the constriction to my chest depriving me of oxygen. It felt like I was wearing a whalebone corset.

That was immediately before the debriefing that provided my introduction to Jordan. But I didn't tell Jeffries about that meeting during my enforced monologue. I took a break, falling miserably silent. I'd accurately recalled my participation in the reconstruction, but that wasn't what he wanted to hear.

'The following day you requested post-mortem photos of a child found dead in Green Park,' Jeffries prompted.

I thought about denying it, but it would have caused trouble for a friend of mine, who'd sent them to me. 'Yes,' I admitted.

'Why?'

It was a fair question and I was sorely tempted to answer. Of course, Chief Superintendent Jeffries already knew the answer. He just wanted me to admit it on tape so he could hang me with it later.

'I thought I recognised the child,' I brazenly lied, fooling no-one.

He ignored me. 'When did you first meet Jordan Lassiter?'

I thought I'd got away without answering that one. Not

that it was the first innocuous meeting he was interested in. It was what followed at my flat the very same evening.

Maybe it had been my concern with the current health and welfare of Celia Potter that had heightened my anxiety. Maybe it had been the fact that I was still unnerved after nearly passing out a few hours before. Or maybe it was because the porch light wasn't working again. But as I approached my front door, I was conscious of a presence. My flat is not located in one of the region's better areas. No upwardly mobile couples would come house-hunting where I live. It offered the intoxicating view of a disused gasworks opposite, that had become home to various illicit nocturnal practices. Although the remaining structures had long been condemned, they were a regular haunt for dealers and junkies seeking their next fix. Abandoned syringes littered the ground and occasionally an addict's body was discovered stretched out on the cracked concrete floors.

My mind raced. What was it we were taught? The worst time to get assaulted was on your doorstep when you had your house keys in your hand. One crack over the head and not only were you physically at the disposal of some sick mind, but they had access to your home and all its contents.

My hand stopped as it approached the keyhole. My heart beat loudly and suddenly there was an unseasonal chill in the air. I wheeled round with my hands raised ready to strike, prepared for anything. All five feet six inches and eight stone of my lithe body was poised.

The shadowy form that detached itself from the bushes was instantly recognisable. Even so, I took an involuntary step backwards. 'Jesus!' I exclaimed as the figure moved closer until the distant streetlights cast a bizarre sodium glow over her features. 'Jordan!'

'We need to talk,' she told me without expression.

'You scared me half to death!' I complained.

Jordan looked one way, studying the street, then the other, observing the garden. 'Why?'

I sighed. It was hopeless. 'You'd better come in.'

As we progressed down the gloomy hall, I asked, 'How do you know where I live?' Receiving no answer, I pushed open my front door and turned on the light.

Jordan stepped over the threshold with a degree of reluctance, casting her eyes around her. Then she turned back, our faces inches apart. 'You've been eating anchovies,' she remarked.

'No!'

She shrugged and walked across the room, studying every object, every trinket and every stick of furniture.

I was still worrying about my breath. 'Yes!' I admitted finally. 'Yesterday. On a pizza.'

She nodded. She might have looked casually dressed, but I recognised the quality of her understated garments. 'Have a seat. I'm going to get changed.'

Having left her alone in the front room, I headed for the bedroom and threw on something more comfortable. When I returned, Jordan hadn't moved. She was standing exactly where I'd left her. She looked like a mannequin, eyes staring straight ahead, focused on nothing in particular. She appeared unwilling to entrust her clothing to my ragged assortment of furniture. It was true; it *had* seen better days.

'Maybe we should go to the pub,' I suggested.

'I don't drink,' she informed me, as though I should have

known.

'Fine! We can go to a coffee shop.'

'I don't take caffeine.'

'Jesus! Where *do* you go?'

Jordan shrugged.

'What do you do when you want to have fun?' I asked in desperation.

'Shoot people.'

It wasn't the answer I'd been expecting. I looked at her impassive face. 'That's a joke, right?'

'Sure,' she replied unconvincingly.

After some persuasion, Jordan agreed to make the short trip to a local pub. We settled around a grimy circular table with a lager and a mineral water. The soiled glasses didn't escape Jordan's minute inspection and she cleaned the rim of hers with a pocket handkerchief. 'So,' I started, trying not to feel intimidated, 'Why would you want to see me?'

Jordan tilted her head to one side. 'Are you not worthy of my attention?'

I sighed. 'I didn't get the impression this was a social call.'

Jordan shrugged. 'I just wanted to see how you were.'

I sighed again. It was one of Jordan's most obvious talents, making people sigh in frustration while in her presence. 'Jordan, I might not know you very well, but I can tell you're lying to me. Why would you do that?'

'Force of habit,' she admitted.

We spent the next few minutes in uncomfortable silence. 'Tell me about the Chinese diplomat,' I suggested. Like everyone else, I'd heard the stories.

Jordan looked up sharply and snorted, then returned her

attention to my dirty glass. I think she was wondering how many previous drinkers could be positively identified from the residue around the rim. The accumulated fingerprints and lipstick could keep the lab busy for a week.

'I guess he had diplomatic immunity?' I prompted, feeling she may already have forgotten the question.

Jordan's shoulders dropped. Once again she gazed at me and once again I was transfixed by those hypnotic eyes: staring straight through me, weighing up my talents and analysing my weaknesses. Boldly, I held her gaze as my pulse steadily rose. Finally, Jordan came to a decision and let loose a long sigh of frustration. 'He also had three gigabytes of photos of himself and various young girls.'

'Oh,' I replied warily.

'His co-stars were very young.'

'Oh,' I repeated. Ramsden had told me a few of the details, but far from everything.

'I still have the discs. You can see them if you want.'

'No. I don't think...'

'They were all encrypted.' Reluctantly, she took a mouthful of mineral water. 'But he volunteered the password... eventually.'

'I wonder how you persuaded him!' I remarked sarcastically.

Jordan shrugged again. 'I can be *very* persuasive,' she told me. Then she took a deep breath. 'They'd just have put him on a plane back to Beijing.'

'So you shot him.' Our eyes met again, but this time I looked away sharply. 'No! Don't tell me. I don't want to know.' I thought about the situation and tried to imagine Jordan taking control of events. It wasn't difficult. I didn't know what I'd have done under the same circumstances. Luckily I wasn't licensed to carry a firearm.

Leaning on the table, taking care not to soil her clothes, Jordan said quietly, 'I need your help.'

'What?'

Jordan looked around her, analysing her question to figure out which part I hadn't understood. 'I need your help,' she repeated slowly.

'Me!'

Jordan sighed. I don't think she could understand why interaction with other people was fraught with so much difficulty. 'I'm told you have outstanding intelligence.'

Like a fool, I fell for it. I was flattered. 'Who told you that?'

'I need the post-mortem photos of the child found dead in Green Park.'

I'd heard about it. Who hadn't? 'The Chinese girl?'

'Yes.'

For the life of me I couldn't understand my significance in Jordan's plans. 'Why do you need me?'

'Because I've asked everyone else and they said no.'

'Ah!' I smiled. 'That's why you went to see Ramsden.' Jordan didn't confirm it. 'It's a different area,' I tried to explain.

'I *need* those photos,' she told me threateningly. 'I've tried everyone!'

I shriveled in my chair trying to disappear.

'So?' she persisted.

'What?'

'I *know* you can get the photos.'

I allowed myself a moment to think. 'Aren't you suspended?'

Jordan took a deep breath. 'You know, I'm *really* trying to like you.'

'That's a great comfort.' I shook my head. 'It's an ongoing investigation. Confidential! And you're suspended! What if I get caught?'

'You'll be suspended as well,' Jordan told me with a half-smile. 'Don't look so glum. We could have a holiday.'

'Holiday!'

'Yuh. I hear Beijing's nice this time of year.'

'Jordan, does insanity run in your family?' I asked in exasperation.

'On my father's side,' she replied casually. 'You remember when I was leaving Ramsden's office? He told me you were on our side. I guess now we'll find out.'

'That's not fair!' I exclaimed. I'd only just met her and already she was trying to drag me down the same shadowy path she habitually trod. 'Look, I'm sure you're used to telling people to do things and they just do them, right? I'm not like that. I need a little more.'

Jordan watched me intently for quite a time before coming to a conclusion. 'I believe the victim in Green Park was one of our Chinese diplomat's co-stars.' She looked up at me and I attempted to fathom whether she was lying to me, again. 'I know for a fact some of them were killed.'

'Is that on the discs?'

'Yes.'

I nodded. Then I did a quick calculation in my head. Jordan might be out of control at times but nobody had ever suggested she wasn't on the side of the angels. 'Okay. I'll get you the photos.'

So, after a fledgling acquaintance of a mere few hours, Jordan had persuaded me to do something irregular, if not strictly illegal. If discovered, it would be a sizeable blot on my personnel record. She had that effect on people. You wanted to please her. The consequences of annoying her were too ghastly to contemplate. She wasn't someone you wanted as an enemy.

I went home, had a long bath and ate one of my mother's 'cook it all in the same pot' meals. Then I felt sick all evening. I could never decide whether her cooking habits owed more to a sense of economy or her irrational fear of aluminium saucepans. Of course, the saucepans weren't made of aluminium anymore, but that didn't stop her worrying.

I sat down in front of the television and tried to relax. As usual, I flicked through multiple channels before finding anything worth watching. I'd just started to get engrossed in a crime drama when the phone rang. I seriously considered not answering, but in the end I gave in. It was my mother with familiar news. 'Your brother's in trouble again,' she told me after the briefest of pleasantries.

I sighed inwardly. 'What is it this time?'

'His wife's thrown him out.'

'Again?' My brother, Trevor, was two years older than me and his marriage was in a state of constant turmoil. In his younger days, he'd fancied himself as a bit of a Casanova, before he finally settled down, supposedly. The recent news of the imminent arrival of their first child didn't make matters any easier. To add to his difficulties, he'd recently lost his job in the City. He'd told our mother that it was the result of a company restructuring, but I guessed otherwise. 'What's he done this time?' I asked.

'Sharon claims she found some photos on his computer.'

It sounded like the same old story. He might be my brother, but my sympathies lay largely with her. 'I think she's just looking for an excuse. I warned him!'

'What do you want me to do about it?' I enquired warily.

'Could you speak to her?'

I remained stubbornly silent. I remembered the last time I'd attempted to mediate between the aggrieved parties: my previously excellent relationship with Sharon had deteriorated into an infantile slanging match. However, a few days later, she'd allowed Trevor to return home. 'I don't think there's much I can do,' I explained patiently. My mother was clearly not impressed with my response and remained silent. 'Where's Trevor now?' I asked.

'He's with your father. Out drowning his sorrows, I should think.'

'Let me speak to Trevor first,' I insisted. 'I'll take it from there.'

'Well, alright then,' she replied, disappointed.

We said our farewells and I headed straight for bed without waiting to discover the identity of the TV murderer.

'When did you first meet Jordan Lassiter?'

God! Jeffries was persistent. He still hadn't got the message I didn't want to answer that one, not honestly anyway. Instead, I told him, 'When it became clear my life was in danger, I asked for her help.'

'Why?'

'Because she's a bodyguard,' I explained.

'But you didn't know her.'

'I'd heard about her.'

'Where did you get her number?'

Good question! It had me stumped, to tell the truth. Presumably, Sergeant Ramsden had informed him of our meeting following the reconstruction, but it would have been highly irregular for her to have passed on her number after such a fleeting acquaintance.

She visited my flat on two consecutive evenings, but the reasons for her visits were subjects too sensitive to discuss with Jeffries. I wanted them to remain private. I remembered meeting Jordan again the following evening; fish and chips immediately came to mind, making me feel hungry. Not that Jordan had eaten any. She only put into her body what she could guarantee was wholesome and natural, unpolluted by chemical additives. And if anybody else had any ideas about inserting anything into her body, they'd better just forget it! She wasn't that type of girl.

I suppose that was one of our many differences. When I thought about it, we had absolutely nothing in common, but it wasn't like we were about to get married. I didn't have any compelling aversion to sex or men in general, especially if the man in question was John Wilson. We were almost a couple when he got caught up in the whole Lawrence Arnold affair. That was long before we ascertained his modus operandi. With a name like John, we'd never have let him anywhere near the action. For Arnold, names were of the utmost importance. Hindsight is a wonderful thing. So was John.

Talking of Arnold's modus operandi, we would later discover that he had strict rules of engagement, beyond which he wouldn't allow his sick mind to operate. For example, he would never target a complete stranger. He'd always made the acquaintance of his victims, however tentatively. He worked as a computer systems operator for a large company up north and was sent on numerous assignments in different areas for different clients. It might be worth pointing out at this time that one of his recent clients had been the Metropolitan Police.

Chapter 3

The story of my 'relationship' with John is littered with false starts and misinterpreted advances. I was attracted to him the first time we met: my second week on the job and the first time our shifts coincided. He had a boyish face with sharp contours and, despite being several years older than me, wouldn't have looked out of place in a sixth-form photo. His foppish fair hair had a tendency to flick across his forehead in an untamed manner and his hazel eyes gave the impression that they were peeping out from under net curtains. Not surprisingly, he was extremely popular.

During my earliest lonely days on the force, John had shown a special interest in me. I thought he was being considerate and taking me under his wing, like a mentor. His mind, as I later discovered, was not working along those lines at all. He was the exception amongst my colleagues in always asking me out for a drink after a shift. It wasn't a big deal: a regular group went two or three times a week. I always declined because I wasn't interested in the places they went. It broke my heart because deep down I thought John was wonderful. I would have happily gone out with him, just the two of us, but he never asked.

After a number of declined invitations, he stopped asking. Nobody likes to bang their heads against a brick wall. Then I had to take the initiative. Whenever I encountered a problem or simply got confused, I always sought him out for advice. Sometimes, we stayed long into the evening in the canteen discussing trivial events of no real significance. We were comfortable together, but he appeared unwilling to instigate anything more than a casual friendship. I knew he was never short of girlfriends, but I wanted to be the one he settled on. What I didn't know was that all the time I was trying to win his affections, he was regularly consorting with a good friend of mine.

So we entered a period of neutrality, when we acknowledged each other but refused to show what we both felt. Anyway, something must have happened in his other relationship, because during the weeks I was assigned to the collator's office, he used every excuse in the book to pay me a visit. It was during this time that we began flirting like schoolchildren. I remember my colleague Cathy giving me a friendly rebuke. Anyone who'd observed us at this point would probably have thought we were an established couple, but nothing could have been further from the truth.

Then came the incident that propelled us together. The uncertainty of our minds was overtaken by a crisis: in the line of duty, John had been the victim of an unprovoked attack by a group of teenage girls, one of whom was armed with an iron bar. She was a big girl! We called her Sumo. He'd called for backup but entered the building before they arrived. When they'd finished with him he had a fractured skull, several broken ribs, severe bruises and lacerations, and unspecified damage to his lower torso, which he refused to discuss with me. I equated 'lower torso' vaguely with the groin area.

Male vanity being what it is, he'd discouraged his friends and colleagues from visiting him. He didn't want them to see what a few schoolgirls had reduced him to. Pathetic really! He'd chosen me as his liaison with the outside world because he knew I wouldn't share his embarrassment with his colleagues. When he was at his worst, it was me he turned to. He'd asked me to bring him a few things at the hospital and I was more than happy to oblige. During the course of a couple of weeks, we'd further developed our friendship.

I visited him just after returning from Celia Potter's flat with Ramsden a day after the reconstruction. We'd searched the place and discovered enough evidence of a protracted campaign against her to thoroughly unsettle me. If ever I was on the end of something like that I'd... Well, I found out soon enough exactly what I'd do.

While I was at the hospital, Jordan was impatiently banging on my front door, but I had no idea at the time.

'Hi!' I said almost apologetically as I entered the sterile cubicle. John had his eyes closed, apparently dozing.

He jerked awake. 'Allison!' he exclaimed as though he was surprised to see me.

'How are you feeling?'

'Better! All better. Cured.'

'Are you?' I responded, surprised.

'Well, not entirely, but they're setting me free tomorrow.'

'Where will you go?'

'Home,' he said simply.

He'd obviously rejected my brilliant idea of recuperating with me. He would need his broken ribs bandaged every day and as luck would have it, I'd taken a relevant first aid course. Naturally enough, I'd offered him my spare bedroom. What he didn't realise was that I didn't have one. We'd have made do, somehow. 'The bandages?' I appealed pathetically.

'We'll work something out,' he said, taking hold of my hand.

I was slightly disconcerted to notice that my mouth

wouldn't close. His gesture was such a simple thing, yet it confirmed the warmth he felt for me. I stared down at my hand in case my senses were playing tricks and deceiving me. He was definitely holding my hand. I didn't have long to enjoy the sensation because suddenly, he pulled away.

'How was your day?' he asked as I imagined us cuddling by the fireplace, and spending our nights together.

'Allison?'

'What?' I asked, startled and somewhat reluctant to interrupt my train of thought.

'You were miles away.'

'Just thinking. What did you say?'

He sighed. 'I asked how you got on today.'

'Oh, Celia Potter. All day!'

'How come?'

'Ramsden has this idea Celia's dead, but can't justify any manpower. Luckily I'm expendable, so I got volunteered.'

'Make any progress?'

'I don't know. We spoke to her parents today, and Eddie Grainger. No-one's confessed yet!'

'What did you make of Grainger?' he asked with a smile.

'I think he liked me,' I reluctantly admitted. Eddie Grainger had been Celia's only serious boyfriend to date. Their relationship lasted some six months before Celia finished it. Grainger was more than a little unhappy with her decision and had generally made a nuisance of himself. Naturally enough, when she went missing, his name was pretty high on the list of suspects. We'd interviewed him at his home. I hoped it was just the physical similarities between Celia and myself that made him leer at me so constantly.

'Good.'

'What's good about it? Mr Potter reckons he's a sexual deviant.'

'Really?' He sounded surprised. 'What gives him that idea?'

'The things he used to make Celia do, apparently.'

'Like what?'

'He didn't specify,' I answered pathetically.

'Didn't you ask?'

I shook my head. 'I didn't want to know.'

'So, what do you think?'

'I've no idea. I was thinking maybe you could help.'

'Because I'm a deviant too?'

'No, because you're a man.' John nodded grimly, eyeing me closely. I shrunk visibly from his glare. 'I got embarrassed,' I muttered.

'Why?'

'I'm not very… you know, experienced with men,' I replied hesitantly.

'Why's that?'

'Take a look at me.'

'Okay, I've done that. Now, are you going to answer my question?'

'Men aren't exactly queuing up for my company,' I admitted.

'I thought that was because you discouraged them.'

'What!?'

'Well, whenever we were going out somewhere after work, I used to ask you along. You were the one who always said no. I guess I just stopped asking.'

'You never went places that interest me,' I explained defensively.

'Like where? What sort of thing interests you?'

'I prefer quiet places: theatre, galleries, museums, that kind of thing. I'm sure you'd all have been thrilled to come along.'

'Hmm... Not all, perhaps. You might be right there. Still, I think I could guarantee the attendance of at least one. You know, I don't particularly like all the noise and chaos of clubs either. I go along because they're my friends and I enjoy spending time with them.'

'So you'd come with me to an art gallery?' I asked with a degree of scepticism.

'Sure, name the day.'

I smiled. 'You're very kind.'

'No, I'm not. I like you. I'd be happy to go somewhere with you.'

I remained unconvinced. 'Which one would you prefer?'

'What about the National? If we're going to start somewhere, it may as well be there. Saturday?'

I nodded, stunned into silence. It sounded as if he was finally asking me out. There had to be some catch. 'Will you be fit?'

'We'll see. Only time will tell.'

On such feeble foundations are the strongest relationships based. However, as relationships go, John and I were not destined to enjoy great longevity. Jordan was unstinting in her contempt for him, rarely sparing my feelings. Her hostility stemmed from a single week years before when they'd worked together. It was difficult to imagine Jordan in uniform but we all have to start somewhere. Neither Jordan nor John wanted to be reminded of those five working days and consequently I struggled to piece together a coherent account of what had happened. I think what it boiled down to was even as a raw recruit, Jordan was reluctant to toe the line. John had apparently complained once too often and found himself handcuffed to the steering wheel while Jordan went to interview some miscreant alone. Within days, one of the major criminal minds of Central London had volunteered a statement incriminating himself in more crimes than you could shake a stick at. He went inside forever and Jordan never told John how she managed it. She later divulged to me the secret of her success and I was torn between admiration and revulsion. Her elevation to CID followed remarkably rapidly.

'Where did you get Jordan Lassiter's number?' Jeffries repeated annoyingly.

I took a leaf out of Jordan's book and looked him right in the eyes while I lied to him. 'Sergeant Ramsden gave it to me.'

'Where was she when you called?'

'I don't know!'

'Why did you need her help?'

'Because I was in danger.'

'What made you think that?'

To understand the answer to that question I have to explain what we found at Celia's flat, together with what we later recovered from her computer. I can only repeat that from the start of this miserable case, I'd been reluctant to get involved. I didn't want to get too close to whatever had happened to Celia Potter. Playing a part in the reconstruction was bad enough, but the following day, Ramsden had me accompany him to her flat. He wanted a female perspective.

That's what he told me anyway.

I soon found out that not only did Celia bear a striking physical similarity to me; her flat was nearly as dim and depressing as mine. It was located in a converted Edwardian property that was probably very nice when it was built. Subsequently, the area had fallen into the sort of typical inner city decay that would preclude any father sanctioning his young daughter living there. Before we even crossed the threshold and entered the Twilight Zone of Celia's life, I discovered three trampled cigarette butts loitering under a threadbare laurel bush: it looked as if someone had been waiting and observing. I reminded myself to check my own front garden. I was already developing a healthy paranoia.

Inside, the flat was a bit of a mess. Well, it wasn't as though she could afford a regular cleaner. And there was an unhappy combination of odours. It was a bedsit with a small area cordoned off as a kitchen. Her bed linen and furniture were spotted with circular holes, fringed with charring: cigarette burns. I looked at them with confusion. I even stuck the tip of my little finger through a couple of them. Ramsden told me Celia didn't smoke and even if she did, I knew several people who appeared to have mastered the technique without incinerating their bedlinen.

Her TV had a cross etched into its screen, in the top left hand corner. It looked like a religious icon, not a plus sign. When we checked the windows, two bore similar crosses, one scratched onto the outside of the glass, the other inside. It was evident that whoever was responsible for the damage had access to Celia's flat. There was no sign of a break in, so they must have had a set of keys. Celia was obviously worried about something because the front door had too many locks and chains. I thought I'd been overcautious at home, but I couldn't match her series of locks.

In the drawer of her bedside table, I found a stack of papers: bills, insurance documents and bank statements: the ordinary paperwork of everyday life. Then I discovered something that was anything but ordinary. Inserted rather conspicuously towards the bottom of the pile was a Polaroid picture. It depicted Celia lying naked on her bed with her legs spread. The photo didn't leave a lot to the imagination. She had a strawberry birthmark in the shape of India on her right inner thigh. Everything I'd been told about Celia rendered this discovery surprising. The people who knew her certainly hadn't given me the impression that she was a potential suburban raver. When I looked closer at the small picture, it was clear that Celia was asleep or unconscious when the photo was taken. Her body was posed limply and her eyes were firmly closed.

I found nothing of interest in the kitchen, until I started rooting around in the rubbish. Torn into several pieces and stained with a combination of cold tea and egg white, was a letter from her credit card company. She'd evidently reported transactions on her statement about which she had no knowledge. The letter informed her that an investigation had been instigated and the police informed.

After that, I went back to the bedside table and checked her bank statements more thoroughly. Her account showed a balance of several thousand pounds, including a recent large deposit. Celia was a student who worked several evenings in a pub to keep the wolf from her door. I couldn't understand where the money had come from. It wouldn't be long before I found out.

I also discovered that someone had set fire to her dustbin, having strategically placed it beneath one of her two windows. One of the windows was filthy, grimy and smeared, the other scrupulously clean. When I'd looked outside, I found a large inverted teardrop of charred brickwork immediately beneath the window, corresponding exactly to the height of the metal dustbin. There was nothing salvageable in the bin, just a few sodden ashes clinging to the base.

I reluctantly turned my attention to the unusual smells in the room. I recognised chlorine: the unpleasant pungent aroma of swimming pools that made my eyes sting and my hair go frizzy. I checked the bathroom, the logical place for a bottle of bleach. There wasn't one. Neither was there one in the kitchen. When I innocently pulled open the wardrobe doors, the stench became overpowering. Her neatly spaced clothes had been ruined. Someone had stood where I was standing and sprayed bleach in sickening waves across her clothes. Their colours had been leached in psychedelic stripes. They were unwearable.

So that was the explanation for the first and most distinctive smell. I could also smell something less tangible, like rotting flesh. It was weak and appeared concentrated around a large linen chest that served as Celia's TV stand. One by one I removed the immaculately pressed sheets from the chest and laid them flat on the floor. The smell grew stronger, yet the bedclothes looked as though they hadn't been disturbed for some time. I removed the last item, a brightly coloured beach towel and stared down at a small cardboard box.

'Oh!' I abruptly rose, my hand involuntarily covering my mouth as the vile smell intensified.

Ramsden moved nearer, not getting too close before peering inside. 'Let's have it then.'

Great! I really didn't want to know what was inside. The box looked like it may have once contained a piece of jewellery. Approximately four inches square, it was constructed of stout cardboard. Reluctantly, I took it in my hands, relieved I was wearing latex gloves. Slowly, carefully, I removed the lid. Inside I saw nothing but a layer of cotton wool. My hands trembled slightly as I took hold of the packing and lifted it up.

At the base was a dead rodent. Lying on its back with its tiny nose in the air, its limbs were outstretched and pinned to a piece of cardboard. It looked like an experiment in school biology. The skin from its neck to groin was slit open and peeled back, revealing its internal organs.

'Disgusting!' I exclaimed with a groan, far from certain what I was looking at. 'Is that a mouse?' I thought it was, but every time I'd previously seen a mouse it had been from the outside.

Ramsden swallowed audibly, nodding. 'It used to be.'

The sergeant busied himself writing in his notebook while I closed the box and placed it in a clear plastic bag. I sat wearily on the edge of the bed looking at the bedside table. It reminded me too much of my own lonely bedroom: a travel alarm clock and a thumbed paperback. The book seemed to be an example of romantic fiction. Evidently another young lady to whom romance was a stranger. I knew exactly how she must have felt. A cheap bedside lamp stood at the edge of the table. I flicked the switch and it sprung instantly to light. I hadn't realised that dusk was drawing in.

The most compelling evidence we found was on the computer, which appeared reasonably new and bore a lead that stretched towards the phone socket. Before turning it on, I checked the phone, discovering that the last calls into and out of Celia's flat were to and from the local police station. Curious.

I sat facing the computer screen and, after ensuring everything was plugged in, pushed the button. Immediately, the whirr of the hard drive started and the tinny speaker offered a beep. I sat back as the machine checked its memory and embarked on its lengthy booting process. Soon, the Windows logo burst to life amidst a blue sky and white clouds. Celia hadn't done much in the way of configuring the machine to her personal preferences. Only one icon was represented on the desktop: a word processor. I clicked on the icon and a familiar application opened. Ramsden stood behind me, observing my progress. Looking in the file menu I checked Celia's most recent documents, calling one up named *Stalker*. The document contained a list of dates on the left. A corresponding list of incidents was offset on the right.

The top entry listed a date some two months earlier, and read *Telephone calls started, silent*. The next entry, made a few days later, read *Harlequin postcard*. I'd just about read the next entry, *Changed telephone number*, when something extraordinary happened: the letters turned fluid and started dripping down the screen.

'What?' I murmured, desperately trying to read further entries. Before I had the chance, the letters had all accumulated in the bottom margin of the screen in an indistinct black bar. Scrolling from the top downwards, the entire screen slowly changed from white to black. We looked on stunned as graphics began to appear. Pixel by pixel, a child dressed as an angel filled the centre of the screen. Her wings were spread wide and her face was upturned in an epiphany of agonised grief. A bright halo appeared, suspended above the angel's head. Then, the image began to move, scrolling right until it rested against the border of the screen. In the space vacated on the left, appeared the word, Martyr.

'What the hell's happening?' asked Ramsden.

I shook my head as the letters started to drip away, turning the colour of blood and accumulating in a sickly pool at the bottom of the screen. 'Some sort of virus?' I suggested, wishing I'd chosen a different career.

At that moment, I had no idea who had posed for the original photo. If anyone had told me then, I'd have laughed in their face. All I could tell from the image was that it had been a young girl, blonde hair, cherubic...

'What first gave you the impression you were in danger?' Jeffries persisted.

I tried to remember the first manifestation of the peril to which I was about to be exposed. It should really have been the neat little cross scratched onto the outside of my kitchen window. Luckily, the net curtain all but obscured it and until I went looking for it days later, I hadn't even noticed it. Good thing really. That was before Arnold upped the tempo and left no-one in any doubt about his intentions.

Growing weary waiting for an answer to what, after all, wasn't an unreasonable question, Jeffries changed tack and tried something different. 'Tell me about Jordan Lassiter. You obviously knew each other before you called her.'

Bastard! Calling me a liar! Just because I wasn't telling the truth was no reason to get offensive. 'I *had* met her briefly before,' I admitted. Confirming a fact he already knew wouldn't cause any problems.

'When?' he demanded unpleasantly.

'She came into Sergeant Ramsden's office during my debriefing.'

'What for?'

'I don't know. I was asked to leave the room.'

'And *she* asked you to get her the post-mortem photos?'

I stopped studying the scratched tabletop and looked up at him sharply. 'No.'

'Tell me about your subsequent meetings.'

Subsequent meetings. Oh yes, there she was banging on my front door while I was fleetingly holding John's hand in hospital.

By the time I reached home, I was exhausted. Visiting John stretched on until the arrival of his parents, when I said hello and diplomatically departed. I think my lethargy was caused at least in part by the fact that I hadn't eaten anything since consuming an inadequate sandwich sometime during the morning. Not having enough energy to cook, I took the long way back from the bus stop, via the fish and chip shop. I slammed the front door and dumped the food on the table. Then I hastily closed the curtains and flicked on the lights. The mixed aroma of fried fish and vinegar filled the small room: a room not unlike Celia Potter's.

I wandered into the kitchen and put on the kettle, throwing the curtains across the small window. Had I not been in such a hurry, I might just have noticed a small cross etched into the pane of glass.

The entry-phone buzzed and I groaned. I was tired and irritable, hungry and fed-up. All I wanted was to eat in peace, have a shower and go to bed. I picked up the receiver, 'Yes!'

'Where the hell have you been!' came the instantly recognisable growl of Jordan Lassiter.

I sighed and pushed the button that opened the front door. I was already tired and just talking to Jordan was a constant trial. It sapped my strength. She breezed in, looking unusually contented, and sniffed the air with a frown, immediately recognising the smell of vinegar. Then she remembered that she should be looking angry. 'I've been waiting hours,' she complained.

'Well, I didn't know you were here!' I exclaimed. 'I went to the hospital on my way home.'

'Are you hurt?'

'No,' I sighed. It might have been my fatigue, but I thought I detected a degree of anxiety in the question. 'I was visiting one of my colleagues. Fractured skull.'

Jordan nodded. She seemed happy enough with the explanation. 'What have you got for me?'

I retrieved an A4 envelope from beneath my wrapped dinner. I'd picked it up on my way out of the station. There's nothing quite so efficient as the Metropolitan Police internal mail service. Several dark patches of grease stained the buff envelope. I handed it over.

Jordan turned up her nose at the sight of it and said, 'Go ahead, eat.'

'You want some?'

Jordan shook her head and sat down. By the time I returned with a plate, she was avidly studying the photos. I sorted myself out and asked, 'Well?'

'Can I use the computer?'

'Yeah, go ahead,' I agreed readily. That was before I started to wonder what she wanted to use it for. I almost lost my appetite when Jordan pulled a stack of CDs from a small bag and slipped one into the tray. I shook my head and chose to ignore her. The less I knew about what was going on the better. My meal was accompanied by a steady clicking of the mouse. Absentmindedly, her left hand stretched out in the direction of my fruit bowl. It was one of those rare occasions when it wasn't empty. She grabbed a mottled banana and without taking her attention from the screen, peeled it and started to eat. Halfway through, she seemed to remember herself and turned sharply to face me. 'Can I have this?' she asked.

'It looks like you already have.' And that's another thing about Jordan: niceties like 'please' and 'thank you' were alien concepts to her. I was once treated to a reluctant 'sorry' but it was pretty obvious she wasn't remotely apologetic.

Ten minutes later, the mouse was still clicking and I stood up to make another cup of tea. Carefully keeping my back to the computer screen, I crabbed my way to the kitchen. 'Tea?' I asked.

'Boiling water.'

Oh, yes. No caffeine. I felt like asking her for the 'magic word' but I didn't want to incur her wrath. She might have hit me.

When I returned, I was delighted to see the screen blank. I handed over Jordan's boiling water, and watched as she inserted a sachet of purple vegetation into it. The water quickly turned an unnatural puce and gave off an aroma that reminded me of compost. 'Look at this,' insisted Jordan and, quicker than I could react, she clicked the screen back on.

'Oh, gross!' I moaned, my stomach threatening to empty again.

Jordan held up one of the post-mortem photos so that everything on the screen was covered except the girl's head. 'What do you think?'

I studied the two images. 'It could be.' The girl was very young. Her rounded face bore unmistakably oriental features, distorted on the monitor by her physical pain. Then Jordan was clicking again and a succession of images flashed on the screen of the pair in various poses. 'Jordan!' I cried. 'I've just eaten!' I sat down in a seat from where I couldn't see the screen as Jordan clicked through a few hundred more depraved photos. 'How many are there?' I asked in desperation.

'Thousands.'

'And you've looked at them all?'

'Most of them.'

'Why?'

Jordan broke her attention away from the monitor and looked at me. 'Know your enemy,' she said simply. 'It also helps to know their victims.' Some minutes later, Jordan found an image that proved her case beyond doubt. 'Look at this,' she urged me.

'I'd really rather not.'

After a brief glance in my direction, Jordan made a note of the file name and closed down the computer, removing the disk. She carefully replaced the photos in their grease-stained envelope and slotted them into her jacket pocket. She stood, arching her back. Slowly, she took a look around her. I figured it was just for effect, there wasn't anything in the room she hadn't already registered. 'You like living here?' she asked, trying to keep the distaste from her voice.

'Not particularly, but I have to start somewhere.'

Jordan nodded slowly, an expression of concern registering on her features.

'Where do you live?' I asked. I didn't really want to know, but Jordan had instigated a conversation and I felt I should attempt to keep it bumping along.

'Hampstead.'

'Very nice.'

She nodded again in confirmation, turning towards the door. Having taken one giant stride, she stopped and suggested, 'You'll have to visit some time.'

I was shocked. 'Are you serious?'

'Yeah, why not?'

'I heard you weren't too sociable.'

'No. I'm just very selective.'

'I'm honoured.'

Jordan smiled. 'Thanks for the photos,' she said. 'I'll be in touch.'

I felt dejected. She had what she wanted and I'd probably never hear from her again, unless she needed something else. I recognised the brush-off. It was hardly the first time it had happened. After all, why would someone like Jordan want to socialise with me? For some reason, I was more disappointed than I'd expected. 'Right!' I got up to let her out.

Jordan turned again. The smile remained on her face. Then she reached out and pressed my nose almost affectionately with her index finger. I just stood there stunned. It was so out of character. 'I'm going away tomorrow,' she told me. 'Abroad. I don't know how long. I'll give you a call when I get back.'

'Where are you going?'

After a brief pause, she responded, 'It's probably better

you don't know that.'

'Okay.'

'Oh!' Jordan remembered. She removed a card from her jacket pocket. 'You need *anything*, give me a call.' She passed me the card standing beside the door looking pensive, reluctant to step across the threshold. 'There's a file on its way to you. You'll get it in the morning.'

I looked up at her, puzzled. Spending time with Jordan was likely to cause a serious crick in my neck. Besides, I was still thinking about her unexpected gesture. And I was on the verge of sneezing. 'Wait! What is it?'

Briefly, she turned back. 'Another *Martyr* file,' she said quietly.

My faced dropped. 'You know something?'

Jordan appeared deep in thought for a long while. I watched, but couldn't make eye contact. She rubbed her chin. 'Bradford. Young girl.'

'Go on,' I urged.

Jordan shook her head. 'Girl in Bradford. I was working on something else at the time.' She stopped to think, attempting to dredge vague memories. 'She died.'

'She was killed?'

'Yes. And her eyes were removed.'

So we had another martyr. I was surprised Jordan had even heard of the case. It had happened several months ago and to my knowledge Jordan had never worked in Bradford. All right, it was an unusual case, but I remember wondering why she'd committed it to memory. There had to be a good reason...

So now you know how I got Jordan's telephone number, which puts you one up on Jeffries, to whom it was still a complete mystery. I didn't want him getting carried away with the idea that Jordan and I were developing a working relationship beyond the confines of approved procedure. Though very soon that relationship would diverge irrevocably from any established course.

'Tell me about the phone calls,' Jeffries asked.

I'll never forget that evening: sitting in my miserable darkened flat all alone listening to my answering machine. That was before I checked my mail...

'I'm not answering anything else until I know how Jordan is,' I told him.

'Anything *else*?' he said with disgust. 'You haven't told me anything yet.'

'And I'm not going to until you tell me how she is.'

He extracted a pristine handkerchief from his trouser pocket and proceeded to blow his nose loudly. It was a theatrical diversion while he made up his mind what to tell me. I didn't think anyone still starched their handkerchiefs. I'm normally a tissue person myself, but when I have a cold, I resort to Egyptian cotton: very soft and it never makes my streaming nose sore.

'Jordan survived,' he told me. Bastard had known all along!

'What about her leg?' When I'd last seen her, her foot had been projecting at a stomach churning right-angle to her leg.

'They decided against amputation. They're going to attempt reconstructive surgery.'

I breathed a sigh of relief. She was going to be okay. But

she would have to embark on a slow and painful rehabilitation. I wondered how she'd react. Her body was an object of immense pride to her. She'd honed it to its limits and maintained a level of fitness that would make a marine envious. For a while at least, she'd be an invalid. I hoped I'd be around to help her recover.

'Tell me about the postcards.'

He had to bring up the postcards! The phone calls were bad enough, but the postcards...

He'd asked what first gave me the impression I was in danger. I hadn't answered him, but now I did. It was a trivial incident that I would normally have written off as a practical joke; I was frequently the victim of such juvenile behaviour.

I'd understandably slept badly the night after Jordan's second visit. I felt pretty ragged the following morning as I clocked in for work. My colleagues were assembling in the duty room. A few early risers were already in uniform, but most were in civilian dress, checking in, chatting idly and wandering in the direction of the locker room. My mood didn't improve when the Duty Sergeant called me over.

'Allison!' he shouted, attracting everyone's attention. 'What are you doing here?'

I looked around as my fellow officers raised eyebrows and lingered to see what was going on. As far as I was aware, that morning was just like any other. 'I work here,' I explained.

'We weren't expecting you today.'

I began to feel a little self-conscious, like I was the target of some elaborate practical joke. 'Why not?'

'You have concussion,' he told me, a concerned look on his face.

'I do?'

'You shouldn't be working.'

Glancing around, I expected to see my colleagues break into beaming grins as the joke was exposed. It wouldn't be the first time they'd shared a laugh at my expense. They all looked on with growing fascination. 'There's nothing wrong with me,' I insisted.

'Your boyfriend called and told me what happened. You should be in bed.'

After a moment to consider the situation, I closed my mouth and asked, 'Why? What *did* happen?'

The sergeant started looking worried, then anxious, as if concerned that the concussion was affecting my memory. 'You stayed at his place last night,' he told me slowly. 'You fell down the stairs and banged your head. You spent hours in casualty. You have concussion. They kept you in overnight for observation.'

By now, quite a crowd had gathered and I felt distinctly embarrassed. Someone must have conducted a practical joke. 'I was at home last night, on my own,' I insisted. 'I didn't fall down any stairs. I live on the ground floor.' I left my explanation there, not wanting to admit that my boyfriend existed only in my dreams.

'Are you sure?' asked the sergeant.

I managed to convince him I was fit for duty. Looking back, maybe it would have been better if I'd just turned around and gone home.

It *was* a trivial incident leaving no indelible scars, but I couldn't help wondering who was responsible. My colleagues wouldn't think twice about playing a prank like that and were probably kicking themselves that they hadn't thought of it first, but they wouldn't have let the joke drag on. They might not have a very high opinion of me but they'd want to gloat. I'm convinced it was Lawrence Arnold. Somehow, he'd discovered that Jordan was paying me visits. It was a warning shot across my bows.

'The postcards?' Jeffries reminded me.

He didn't give up! The postcards. We soon learned that the simple postcard was Lawrence Arnold's favoured method of communication. Not scenic postcards, but images of tortured souls and martyred saints drawn from Renaissance paintings. He didn't write anything on them. He didn't need to. The picture itself was the message.

Jeffries was asking me to describe the effects of being the recipient of one of these cards, as unfortunately, I was. Even more unfortunately, I was later the recipient of several others, each of which had portrayed a scene of which I'd rather not be reminded. All except one. You might remember that one of the few items I'd managed to discern from the schedule on Celia's computer read *harlequin postcard*. That was before the letters melted away and the angel appeared. A harlequin postcard may sound inoffensive enough, but Celia had obviously thought it played a part in the escalating campaign against her.

Chapter 4

The day after our search of Celia's flat, I was expecting to be back pounding the beat. I would have welcomed anything to distract me from the spectre of Celia Potter. However, it wasn't that easy. That morning, I'd received the file on Lucy Falkus, the girl from Bradford who'd been murdered and whose eyes had been none too skillfully removed. The conversation I'd been party to with a sergeant in Leeds had left a very sour taste in my mouth.

I wasted no time passing the file to Ramsden. I watched as he read with moderate interest, stifling a yawn at one point. It was only towards the end, when he encountered the familiar image of a golden-haired child portraying an agonised angel that his face dropped. By the time the *Martyr* image appeared, he had the phone in his hand. A hasty series of calls later, the two of us were speeding up the M1 in the direction of Yorkshire in the very same Ford Mondeo that would later be stationed outside Jordan's flat. When we arrived, there was no inspector available, the case was on the back-burner awaiting developments, but we managed to hook up with a sergeant who was familiar with the case.

DS Woodstock was a force veteran, accustomed to his rank and unlikely to rise higher. A blunt Yorkshireman, he was overweight, divorced and exceedingly irascible. His thinning grey hair was tinged with the yellow glow of a lifelong smoker. In these days of enlightened anti-smoking legislation, his unrequited cravings added to his mood of despondency and he looked permanently aggrieved. His hands twitched uneasily. No pen or pencil was left unchewed in his search for a cigarette substitute. Ramsden and I faced him across a desk in a modern office little bigger than a toilet stall. Woodstock was forced to squeeze his bulk between the desk and the wall to assume his chair. He pointedly addressed his comments to Ramsden. Conversing with a lowly constable, female to boot, was apparently beneath his dignity.

'Yeah, we struck lucky,' Woodstock informed us in a broad Yorkshire dialect. 'The pathologist toyed with the idea of becoming a priest in his youth. Fortunately for us, he learned the error of his ways.' He looked at me, catching me by surprise. 'Are you Catholic?' he demanded suddenly.

'My parents are,' I replied in a hushed whisper. If his intention was to intimidate me, he was succeeding.

'What does that make you?'

'Agnostic,' I replied quietly.

He regarded me with a frown before continuing. 'Saint Lucy.' He delved into a blue folder and pulled out a dark photo. 'The quality's not much good but you can just about make her out.' He handed the photo to Ramsden, who proceeded to hold it between us. 'According to the legends, she was martyred in Syracuse. In Sicily,' he added unnecessarily, for my benefit. 'Supposedly, during the persecution of Diocletian. She rejected some chap's advances and he denounced her as a Christian. Not a nice thing to do; not in those days.'

'What happened?' asked Ramsden warily.

'Well, since she valued her chastity so highly, the governor consigned her to a brothel. Somehow she managed to preserve her virginity. The story goes she plucked her eyes out to become less attractive to the punters. Anyway, she obviously wasn't a very good whore, so they set fire to her. She didn't die, so some soldier stabbed her in the neck with a spear.' He shrugged. 'It's probably all bollocks. There's no evidence she ever existed. Some religious types reckon her eyes were miraculously restored after she pulled 'em out. Waste of time I would have thought, she'd probably only have done it again. Anyway, however many eyeballs she had, she's commonly shown holding them on a tray in front of her. That's a picture of an icon from a church in Syracuse.'

'There she is,' mumbled Ramsden.

'Yeah.'

'And Lucy Falkus's injuries were consistent with the legend?' I asked.

Woodstock ignored me and addressed his reply towards Ramsden. 'Her eyes were taken out and the burns inflicted while she was alive, but the wound to the throat killed her. The burns were worst lower down, but there were lesser burns all the way up to her groin, like she was standing in a fire and the flames licked on up. There's pictures.' He sorted through the file, withdrew a buff envelope and extracted several colour shots. Ramsden leafed through them and passed them to me. Feeling increasingly queasy, I studiously avoided looking at them. A brief glimpse of the blackened, blistered skin of Lucy's feet was all the confirmation I needed. I placed the pictures back on the desk. 'There's also evidence that she was sexually abused. She was no virgin! Anyway I've made a copy of everything for you,' explained Woodstock.

'What about the place she was found?' Ramsden went on.

'Far as we know it's an old hunters' hide. It's built into the side of a hillock, part cave, you know. It's in the middle of nowhere. We're lucky anyone found her. She could have been there for months.'

'But she wasn't killed there?' I asked.

'No. No way. There was no blood. The bastard just posed her neatly and left her.'

'Posed how?' I asked.

'There's pictures,' he informed me, before taking a deep breath. 'She was sitting in a chair with a silver tray on her lap with her eyeballs on it,' he explained.

'This hide,' Ramsden continued. 'Could a car have got close?'

'Four-wheel drive. It's all in the file.' He opened it again and leafed through the pages until he came to a halt. 'These are screen prints of the 'Martyr' logo on her computer. Ring any bells?'

'Uh-huh,' confirmed Ramsden as he recognised the image. There were three prints in total, taken as the letters turned to blood and dripped down the screen. 'It's the same.'

'Looks like we've got a killer on the loose.'

'You didn't find any other examples of the virus?' I asked hopefully.

'No. We contacted several computer consultants and experts. None of them had ever heard of anything quite like it. What's your girl's name?'

'Celia Potter.'

'Hold on.' Woodstock proceeded to make a phone call, punching out a number from memory. After several minutes, he was put through. 'Bill? I want to pick your brains. Remember Saint Lucy?' Ramsden and I both heard the loud exclamation from the tiny earpiece. The man called Bill, who I assumed was the pathologist Woodstock referred to earlier, continued for some time in strident tones. 'Can you do me a saint called Celia?' Woodstock asked. A cold chill passed down my spine as I heard the indistinct voice intone for some time between loud chuckles. Finally, Woodstock thanked him, ended the call and turned his attention back to Ramsden. 'Saint Celia, or more commonly Saint Cecelia, the virgin martyr. Not a very happy story. She was broiled in a steam room and...'

'Broiled?' I queried.

'In a Roman bath room, I don't know. Apparently the furnaces were turned up full and she was steamed to death. Only she didn't die. Far too holy for that! So they cut off her head. Only they couldn't. Story goes they tried three times and couldn't chop it off: died from her wounds three days later.'

'Oh, boy!' I muttered. I couldn't help myself. That was immediately before a glaring inconsistency struck me. 'Wait a minute. Both these saints, Lucy and Cecelia died virgins, right?'

'Allegedly. It was terribly fashionable at the time,' he replied in a patronising tone as his gaze flirted down my uniform.

I crossed my legs and asked, 'But you said Lucy was sexually abused.'

'True!' he said, his eyes bright. I was becoming increasingly uncomfortable. He flicked through the file before continuing, 'Her body showed signs of prolonged brutality, tearing and dilation,' he mused, sitting back.

'How does that fit in, then?' I asked, attempting to appear undaunted.

He shrugged. 'Whoever we're dealing with presumably didn't want to waste a gilt-edged opportunity. Lucy must have been held captive for days, anything up to four weeks.

The pathologist wasn't sure about her time of death: her body was in pretty bad condition. He estimated that she'd already been dead for two weeks when she was found, but there's a high margin for error. Anyway, how many women consigned to a brothel remain virgins? Even the ugly ones must have some takers, especially if they're cheap. Besides, some men prefer ugly women.' Again he looked me up and down. His meaning was pretty clear.

'And never a sniff of a suspect?' asked Ramsden.

Woodstock shook his head, scrunching up his nose. 'Nothing.'

This was before we'd identified our own 'suspect'. The name Lawrence Arnold meant nothing to us at that time.

While I took my turn driving, Ramsden studied the contents of the file on Lucy Falkus. It was a very sombre trip back to the station. The file was pretty thick and gave every indication that the investigation had been comprehensive. However, it had floundered through lack of witnesses and viable suspects. As with Celia, Lucy disappeared on a perfectly normal day, while she was walking to college. Two evenings a week, Tuesday and Thursday, she studied Business Management. One moment she was exchanging pleasantries with her neighbours, the next she was gone.

The pathologist's opinion was that Lucy had been 'more dead than alive' by the time she received the fatal blow. She had been burned by cigarettes and her left shoulder and wrist had been dislocated. In addition, the skin of her left wrist had been roughly abraded towards her hand. The theory was that she had spent a lengthy period suspended by a rope around her wrist. There were also signs that her right ankle had been tied to her right wrist. Despite the charred state of her feet, her left heel bore conical scars through to the bone. Numerous other wounds had yet to be explained. It was impossible to fathom the psyche of the killer, the report concluded.

My head was spinning. So much pain, so much mutilation. I began to feel nauseous as I flicked through the crime scene photos again. She'd changed from a fresh-faced college girl to an urban martyr at the whim of some disturbed maniac.

The pathologist and the Yorkshire police had failed to 'fathom the psyche of the killer' because of a simple lack of information. Had they concentrated on the injuries inflicted on Lucy prior to her death, the rope burns to her wrist and the conical wound to her heel, they just might have begun to penetrate the perpetrator's rationale. Someone on their team would have had to be well-versed in the instruments of medieval torture to do so.

Chapter 5

The day after our Yorkshire expedition I was back on the beat. Pounding the streets wasn't my idea of a good time. I'd much rather have been driving around in a warm panda car but I had an uncanny knack of drawing the short straw. I was partnered with a girl called Lydia whose most pressing concern was the acquisition of some fancy new underwear at a swanky boutique in the High Street. By the time we'd wandered half a mile from the station, I knew far more about her love life than I was comfortable with.

The discussion concerning Lucy Falkus was still playing on my mind. I found it difficult not to think of the two girls, one missing and the other dead, without recalling details of the photos of Lucy. I could only imagine her pain as the flames licked up her legs, consuming her flesh. I thought of a pig on a spit and the acrid odour of singeing flesh. I tried not to wonder whether Lucy had been conscious as her skin started to blister and roast. Suddenly, Celia's plight looked pretty hopeless. If the same man was responsible, chances were she would currently be enduring a similar fate.

'Excuse me!'

Something hard thumped into my stomach, temporarily knocking the wind out of me. When I looked down, I saw a small boy sitting on the pavement. 'Allison!' exclaimed my partner and bent to help the child to his feet.

'I'm sorry, I didn't see you,' I explained as tears started welling on his face. I wondered where his mother was. I knelt down beside him. He couldn't have been much older than seven or eight. 'Are you okay?'

His face reflected his growing composure as he nodded. 'Yes,' he answered with a smile.

'So, what can we do for you?'

His face turned to the row of shops under an assortment of colourful awnings. 'A man over there,' he shook his head as he tried to find him, 'He asked me to give you this.' He held out a small card.

'Thank you,' I responded automatically. One glance was all it took to strip the smile from my face. It depicted a man on tall stilts, like someone from a circus. He was part of a parade making its way along a street lined with waving people. His hands were held out and suspended above them was a spinning top hat, which he was evidently juggling. My mouth went dry as I realized that he was dressed in a harlequin costume. I took hold of the child's shoulder. 'Which man?'

The boy took another look at the parade of shops. 'He was there,' he told me pointing towards the corner.

'What did he look like?' I asked, more eager now.

'He was old. He walked with a limp.'

'Get a description,' I shouted to my startled partner as I took off round the corner as fast as I could, running recklessly and narrowly avoiding a pile of boxes stacked for the binmen. I looked down the street, but saw only a black woman pushing a pram and two teenagers holding hands. No! There was someone else: someone in a grey jacket walking away from me, some hundred yards down the street on the opposite side. I started sprinting, barely looking as I flew across the road. The person appeared to be in no particular hurry, walking casually with no discernible limp. My lungs started to ache as I drew in deep breaths, travelling as fast as

I could. As I drew closer, I shouted, 'Stop! Police!'

And a girl turned round.

Shit!

Panting, I returned to my partner, who was still standing with the child.

'Anything?' she asked me.

I shook my head, trying to recover my breath. 'No.' I took a few more deep breaths. 'Have you got a description?' I asked.

'Yeah, but it's pretty vague.'

'Call it in. We need to find him.'

'Can I ask why?'

'Because he's already killed one girl and abducted another.'

By now, the boy's mother's had appeared and her mouth dropped open as she looked at the child. She put her arms around his shoulders and led him away. 'You got the kid's name, right?' I asked.

'Yeah.'

As the call was radioed in, I got the distinct impression that close by, someone was laughing at me.

I guess that was the start. I remembered the small black letters reading 'Harlequin postcard' turning fluid and starting to dribble down Celia's computer screen. I'd assumed that in her case the card had been delivered by post, but we hadn't found it in her flat. So, fairly naturally, I started to worry. Somehow I was in danger of being caught up in the whole thing and I didn't even share a name with a saint. Just to be on the safe side I checked if there had ever been a Saint Allison in the library while we were on patrol that day. *The Wordsworth Dictionary of Saints* didn't have one listed. I breathed a little easier.

'How did John Wilson become involved?'

I smiled briefly at Jeffries' mention of John, before recalling the night at the 'safe house'. My smile abruptly disappeared.

John and I made it to the National Gallery the weekend after his release from hospital. I'd been looking forward to it so much, but when it finally happened my mind was already transfixed by the spectre of the postcard and phone calls. I made it my business not to tell him about them. I didn't want him worrying. He had enough to concentrate on just getting better. In the end, everything went horribly wrong. Let's start with the terrible evening when all my fears and suppositions were confirmed; the night when everything became very personal. It was cold, dark and I felt very alone. I was tired after a day on the streets and just wanted to get to bed.

It was late by the time I returned home. The day had been dry and humid until the moment when thunder and lightning had relieved the tension. When I finally passed through the battered gate that led to my flat, a solitary flash of lightning illuminated the front garden, accentuating the dark caverns lurking beneath the familiar bushes. I checked the shadows: no sign of Jordan tonight. I felt a twinge of disappointment.

I studied the façade of the house as I approached the front door. Everything looked perfectly normal. I couldn't see my own flat from the front, but lights burned behind thick curtains on the first floor. The developers who converted the once imposing Edwardian house had split the ground floor into two equal flats. Mine was located at the back of the house. I picked up two pieces of mail and a postcard from the table in the hall. I could barely read my name: the hall light was broken again.

Inside my flat, I flicked on the main light, my eyes stinging with the intensity. The red neon light was flashing on my answering machine. The machine was a present from my mother who'd never come to terms with the nature of my shift work. Tired of receiving no answer, at least now she could talk to a recording. I drew the curtains, their lining torn and flapping loosely. I hit the button on the answering machine and sank into an armchair to study the post.

'You have three messages,' the machine informed me in stilted tones, before bleeping and rewinding.

I discarded the first envelope, a flier for a low cost credit card from my bank. I already had a credit card I was terrified of using. Money was tight, but I could at least take comfort from the fact that I didn't owe anything to anyone.

The machine wound the tape and started to play. Seconds passed in a hiss of background noise. The message dragged on for half a minute before the call was terminated. I sat up as the machine informed me the call had been made at 3:32 that afternoon. I hadn't changed the clock after British Summer Time ended, so the call had been made an hour earlier, or later for that matter.

The second envelope was also from my bank and I recognised the format of the contents: my monthly statement. I put it to one side, intending to take a look when I had more strength. That turned out to be a foolish oversight, but I wouldn't discover that until later. I'd been with the same bank for four years and they'd never made a mistake. All I wanted to do was relax.

As the second message started playing, I kicked off my shoes. The message was exactly the same as the first. I stared at the machine and concentrated on the unremitting hiss. There was no evidence of anyone on the line. Not even a background of faint breathing: just static. A loud click signalled the end of the recording. The call had been made at 4:38, just over an hour after the first. I sat very still awaiting the third message, toying with the postcard in my hands. My eyes didn't leave the machine as I listened to the tape spinning, locating the correct position. When the third and last message started, I was initially relieved to discover it was different, but as the high-pitched whistling commenced, I recognised a modem seeking an electronic response. The tone of the whistling changed constantly as, not receiving the anticipated reply, it repeated its introduction. After it was satisfied that there was no device at my end to 'shake hands with' it disconnected. I was left listening to a dialling tone.

I sat stationary for some time after the answering machine revealed that the call was made at 5:44. 'That was your last message,' it confirmed. My hand stretched out to press the 'save messages' button but the rest of my body didn't follow. 'I will cancel your messages,' it told me. Still I didn't move. The messages would remain on the tape until they were recorded over.

I knew I should press 1471 and discover from where the last call had originated. I could hear my heart beating in my chest, altogether too fast, too loud. Despite the flat's warmth, I felt cold, chilled. Unwilling to move, I looked down at the card between my index fingers. It was long, about twice the size of a normal tourist postcard. I'd assumed it was just another advertising flier, begging me to drink at one of the local theme bars. Now I saw it was different. The picture was too dark, too bland. No advertising manager would select it.

It didn't grab your attention. I held it at arms' length, studying its full height. It depicted a young lady, her face a uniform porcelain white. Black eyes stared out above an indistinct nose and bold red pinched lips. Her forehead was large and out of proportion. On either side of her face, concealing her ears, flowed cascades of curly ginger hair. Her chin tapered away to nothing, dying into her neck. She was clad in a sumptuous gown with an ebony waistcoat surmounting a scarlet skirt. Her contrived posture suggested an incipient pregnancy, but the white dove perched with its wings outstretched on her right wrist indicated chastity. A crown of some sort circled the top of her head, rather like a halo. Her demeanour was one of tranquility and acceptance.

I rotated the card in my trembling fingers. The back contained a brief description of the painting and my address on a printed label. There was no stamp, no postmark to reveal where it had been posted. The card had not been sent through the post. Someone had hand-delivered it to my door. I held it closer to my face, reading the small print:

Saint Cecilia
by Master of the Diptych of Brunswick:
Rijksmuseum, Amsterdam

There was no message. Whoever delivered the card knew the picture was enough. The chance of there being any of the perpetrator's fingerprints was minimal. Someone in the house had plucked it from the mat and I'd just spent the last couple of minutes fingering it. Slowly, as if it were a bomb waiting to explode, I placed it on the table on top of my two letters. I stood, dazed, and walked to the window that faced the garden. With a swift flick of my arm, I pulled back the curtains and studied the glass. My heart dropped as I noticed the neat cross scratched into its upper corner. I traced the outline with my finger. There was no indentation on the inside. The scratches were outside. Somehow that made me feel slightly better.

I flung the curtains back across the window, blotting out the cross. There was a November chill in the air and my mind was struggling to function. I didn't know what to do. A gnawing sensation filled my stomach and I felt bilious. Within seconds, I was retching and racing for the toilet. I retched until the entire contents of my stomach were deposited. Then I retched some more.

Having washed my face and swilled my mouth out with water, I returned to the front room. Lowering myself gently into an armchair, I brought my hands to my face and began to cry.

That was some night.

Eventually I called Sergeant Ramsden. I couldn't think what else to do. It was painfully obvious when he arrived that he'd been drinking and shouldn't have been behind a steering wheel. I didn't know who else to call. At the time I never even thought of calling Jordan. She told me she was going away, which turned out to be true because when I eventually came to my senses and did contact her, she was in Rotterdam, having conveniently 'forgotten' to inform our Dutch colleagues of her suspension.

I spent the night at the section house, a rectangular concrete annex to the station. There was a guard at the door and I felt a little safer. I still couldn't sleep. When I arrived at the station the following morning, I looked wretched. I didn't feel a lot better when I was ushered directly into Detective Inspector Garratt's office. CID were on the case and they had some catching up to do.

'I believe you received the harlequin postcard first?' Jeffries queried.

'That's right,' I admitted.

Even I was finding the lengthening periods of silence irritating, so I told him about my receipt of the card, after the small boy headbutted me in the stomach. I had to tell him something.

You may have detected the merest trace of antipathy in my attitude towards Chief Superintendent Jeffries and you may be wondering why. After all, he was my senior officer. The truth is: he and Jordan went way back. In his secondary capacity as investigator of police misconduct, it was inevitable he'd run into her sooner or later. He'd conducted a previous enquiry into her behaviour, at the end of which he recommended her dismissal. She had enough friends in high places to ward off the threat, but his reappearance in her life was unwelcome to say the least.

Jordan never told me much about what happened on that first occasion. I only know what I've been told by colleagues. A couple of years ago, while she was on secondment somewhere in Birmingham, she met Tamsin, a tall Indian lady who's one of the few women I know who can look Jordan in the eye without straining her neck or standing on a box. Tams had been similarly reckless in her youth and the pair formed a strong bond. However, marriage and a young child had blunted Tams's indiscretions and she'd become a highly respected officer. I can only assume her brain must have been taking a vacation when she decided Jordan would make a suitable godmother for the child. Anyway, they were still close and we'd have occasion to be thankful for Tams's presence later in the story.

A girl had died. She was the fiancée of a suspect Jordan and Tams had collared after a high-speed chase up the M1 from Birmingham. It appeared pretty straightforward: he was driving a stolen BMW whose boot was crammed with the resultant goodies from the burglary. He'd been on his way to Leeds where his fiancée lived. Understandably, Jordan and Tams decided to make the journey and interview her. This is where details become sketchy but it is said that the girl, short and slight though she was, had approached the towering Jordan in a menacing manner armed with a kitchen knife. During the resulting scuffle the girl incurred a head injury. She died three weeks later of a brain haemorrhage. Fortunately, no-one could conclusively link the two incidents, so Jordan remained on the force despite Jeffries' best efforts.

'What was John Wilson's first involvement?' Jeffries had a list of questions written on a single sheet of A4. He was acting like a schoolboy in an exam, trying to shield the writing with his forearm.

And then we were there...

John and I emerged from the underground station with the imposing façade of the National Gallery ahead of us. After much soul-searching, I'd decided to keep my date with him, even after a sleepless night in the section house. Tourists posed for photos on the famous steps while pigeons scrounged scraps and pickpockets mingled surreptitiously with the crowd. An occasional uniformed bobby wandered through the scene, and huge red double-deckers circled the square.

John was okay, although climbing steps tired him after weeks of inactivity. His face was slightly flushed and a few beads of perspiration dappled his brow. He insisted on wearing a red baseball cap to conceal his shorn scalp and ugly stitches. Frankly, I didn't care how he looked. He was with me. I hadn't told him anything about what was happening: the phone calls, the postcard or the scratches on my window.

We hadn't got as far as the entrance before I received my first shock. Being short of cash, I queued up behind a ragged assortment of tourists to make a withdrawal from a nearby machine. I had money at my flat, but I hadn't wanted to go back there alone. When it was my turn, I began by requesting my account's balance. I was always careful with money because my family never had enough. I'd learned good financial housekeeping at an early age. Every month I kept just enough cash in my current account and deposited the rest in my savings account. I was often desperate by the end of the month, but so far I hadn't ever touched my savings. The day I met John was close to the end of the month and I faced the possibility of the machine bluntly refusing my request for cash.

I was still looking puzzled when I rejoined John, who was standing towards the rear of the queue.

'What's up?' he asked.

'I have too much money,' I replied, still examining the slip.

'Terrible!'

His voice was loaded with irony, but I didn't find the situation funny. I was worried. The slip told me I had over twelve hundred pounds in my account, which wasn't possible at that time of the month. We wouldn't be paid until the following week and besides, the last time I withdrew cash, I had less than one hundred pounds. Not wanting to sour the day, I slotted the slip into my purse and tried to forget about it. It was one more thing to pass onto DI Garratt.

John was smiling at me as we made our way at snail's pace towards the entrance. 'Okay?' he asked.

I returned his smile. Everything else could wait. 'Sure!' I assured him and took hold of his arm.

As we started to climb the steps, I reminded myself to take them slowly. John hadn't regained his fitness and I didn't want him tired so early in the day. Little by little, our arms slid progressively down, gradually unlocking until our hands touched. John took the initiative and grasped my hand, interlocking his fingers with mine. I felt a flush of contentment work through my body and when I looked up at him, he smiled and pushed a stray strand of my hair back behind my left ear. His touch was electric.

The day passed in a blaze of pent-up emotions. We wandered from room to room studying the paintings, but concentrating on each other. The gallery was crowded, but we didn't notice. All the other spectators were just extras in our personal movie. After a couple of hours, John felt tired. We went to the cafeteria and had a sandwich and a cup of tea. Refreshed, we returned to the galleries. I'd promised his parents we'd be back early, but when the afternoon was thinking of becoming evening, he suggested we go for a meal.

Most restaurants had yet to open, but we found places catering for the all-day tourist trade around Leicester Square. By the time we settled on Greek food, John was about ready to collapse in his chair. He puffed out his cheeks. His face was red and those droplets of perspiration were back. But he was still smiling and I was still the centre of his attention.

His injuries hadn't affected his appetite. We ate a lot! I was starving. John couldn't drink alcohol, but who needed artificial stimulants? I was already intoxicated. When we received the bill, John prepared to pay. I stopped him. 'I'll take care of it.'

He looked reluctant. 'On one condition.'

'What's that?'

'I'll pay next time.'

'Okay,' I replied, trying to hide my excitement that he was contemplating a next time.

My delight abruptly turned to embarrassment when the curly haired waiter returned and informed me that my credit card had been rejected.

'That's not possible!' I exclaimed. I looked at the card lying forlornly on the silver tray. 'It's valid for another two years.'

'I double checked,' he said. 'Your card was cancelled two days ago.'

'I haven't cancelled it.'

'That may be so but I cannot accept it.'

Reluctantly, I dug out my debit card. Since I had so much money in my current account, I might as well use it, even though I didn't know where it came from.

John had reached inside his jacket and removed his wallet, but I impatiently waved away his proffered card. 'Is everything all right?' he asked.

I shook my head. I remembered the letter I'd found in Celia's rubbish bin. Someone was fraudulently using her credit card and she'd also discovered an unexpectedly high balance on her bank statement. It was all a bit too close for comfort and tears welled in my eyes. 'No,' I said simply.

When the waiter returned and asked me to sign on the dotted line, John asked, 'Can we have another coffee, please?'

After a moment's hesitation, he grabbed the five-pound note. 'Certainly, sir.'

Over coffee, I revealed the whole depressing story, despite having promised myself I wouldn't burden him. 'Now there's something going on with my accounts. I didn't cancel my credit card and I shouldn't have twelve hundred pounds in my current account. God knows what's happening in my savings account!'

There was nothing John could say to put my mind at rest. What he'd just learned worried him nearly as much as it worried me. Instead, he reached across the table and covered my hands with his. 'Sorry, I had no idea.'

'I didn't want you to know!' I exclaimed, still fighting back tears. 'I don't know what to do. Inspector Garratt wants me to go back to the flat and just sit there and wait.' I looked up at him. 'I'm scared.'

He thought for a moment, sipping his coffee. 'A while ago you offered to put me up while I recuperated. Does the offer still stand?'

'No!' I replied quickly. 'I can't. Not now.'

'Why?'

'Because you're not fit. What if something happens?'

'Then... I'll call for backup.'

That was a good one! I shook my head. 'No, you wouldn't. You'd try to do something yourself. You know you would.'

He smiled. 'Well, maybe. But wouldn't it make you feel safer having someone around?'

'Of course.'

'Well, then.'

'What would you tell your mother?'

'Ah! That could present a problem.' After a moment's thought, he lifted both of my hands to his mouth and kissed them. 'I know! I'll tell her I've fallen madly in love and can't bear to spend another second without you.'

'Yeah, right! She's going to believe that.'

'Why not?' he asked innocently.

'She's more likely to ask what the hell you see in me,' I remarked, looking down at the chequered tablecloth.

'Well, in that case, I'd have to tell her.'

I didn't bother looking up. I was too confused. 'Tell her what?'

'What I see in you.'

A mischievous smile threatened to flicker at the corners of my mouth. 'And what's that?'

He exhaled audibly. 'Well, I don't know really. It's something to do with being delicate, almost fragile. You're a bit like a... I don't know, a snail. If anyone's too rough with you, you might break.'

I wasn't entirely impressed by the analogy.

So, that was my first date with John. There wouldn't be many others. I suppose some people might think that being likened to a mollusc wasn't very flattering, but he meant well. And he'd agreed to babysit me. He was far from fit, but I couldn't think of anyone I'd rather have by my side.

Chapter 6

The following day I thought differently. What was I thinking? John was recovering from a fractured skull, broken ribs and as yet unspecified groinal damage.

We managed to convince John's parents that nothing untoward was going on and that he'd be safe as houses with me, though we were far from certain that was true. They looked on sullenly as he packed an overnight bag. I had to blush when he told them he would be sleeping in the spare bedroom.

A surveillance team was set up opposite the front of my house to monitor comings and goings. Unfortunately, since my flat was at the rear of the house, they couldn't see it. There was another team covering the rear in an adjoining street, but because the two rows of houses were almost perpendicular, they were a long way away. They didn't have a very good view.

I told Garratt all about my bank accounts and he said he'd look into it. I thought he looked worried, but he tried not to show it.

So there we were, installed in my flat. After a day wandering around the National Gallery, John was fit to drop and he did just that. He sat in a chair and while I was making a cup of tea, he fell asleep. I woke him a little later and tried to usher him into the bedroom.

'Why?' he asked in a hoarse voice. 'I'm happy here.'

'You're sleeping in the bed,' I told him firmly.

'I thought you had a spare room.'

'What on earth gave you that idea?'

'You told me when I was in hospital.'

'You must have been delirious,' I told him.

His eyes were fully open, although sleep still shrouded his features. He stretched his arms wide and exhaled. His arm found my shoulder and a gentle tug overbalanced me into his lap. 'Ow!' he groaned. "Serves you right!" I thought as I tried to remove my weight from his injured ribs. He pulled my head to his chest and held me there, stroking my hair tenderly. Softly, he kissed the top of my head and then sat back, sleep overcoming him.

It took me about half an hour to extricate myself from John's embrace. Not that I was trying too hard, but my twisted muscles had become a mass of aches and pains. I took a lingering look at his relaxed features, listening to his slow breathing. The spectre of Lawrence Arnold seemed a very long way away.

I tiptoed across the room and grabbed the telephone. It was still relatively early, although I was tired after a difficult day. I called my parents. As usual, my mother answered promptly. After the usual pleasantries, I got down to business. 'Is Trevor there?'

'No, he's out with some friends,' she told me. 'Have you spoken to Sharon yet?' she demanded.

'No, I told you, I want to speak to Trevor first,' I reminded her.

'Well, don't leave it too long,' she urged. 'He went back to collect some clothes yesterday. She wouldn't let him in!'

I groaned. Time may well be a great healer, but Sharon was evidently badly hurt. 'I'll do what I can,' I assured her.

Finally, I plunged the room into darkness and got ready for bed. I hadn't expected to sleep in the bedroom for a while. John was an invalid with two broken ribs, but he'd insisted on taking the armchair. Thinking fondly of my new houseguest, I fell asleep.

'Tell me about John Wilson.' Jeffries insisted.
   'He came to stay at the flat,' I told him.
   'And what happened there?'
   'Nothing!' I replied indignantly.
   He sighed. 'I mean in relation to the case.'
   'Oh! Nothing. Not that night.'

Nothing happened but I had a hell of a shock when I woke up the next morning.

Bright sunlight flared through the thin curtains, creating abstract patterns on the wall. I forced my eyes open and took a deep breath to greet the morning. I felt unusually hot and I was sweating. It was shortly after nine in the morning, and after a brief moment, I realised it was Sunday. I rolled onto my back and propped myself up on my elbows. I couldn't stop a broad smile crossing my face as I remembered the previous evening. John was in a chair sleeping in the room next door. The smile abruptly disappeared as I looked towards the door and noticed him lying right next to me, his eyes staring at me, looking guilty.

A brief shriek left my mouth before I realised it was coming. Despite the cotton T-shirt that covered my upper body, I immediately clenched the sheets and pulled them up to my chin.

'Morning,' he mumbled.

My mouth opened but I found myself lost for words.

'Sorry,' he said sheepishly. 'I woke up in agony. I had to

lie down.'

'Right,' I mumbled, holding the sheet very tightly.

'Sorry,' he repeated.

I took a deep breath, my senses still swimming. 'It's okay,' I said after a moment's hesitation. 'I should have slept on the sofa. I was planning to.' We lay there silently, neither knowing quite what to do. After a lengthy silence, I added, 'I was going to get up.'

'Okay.'

I looked at him, waiting.

'What?' he asked.

I indicated my body, concealed beneath the covers. 'Do you mind?'

'Oh! Right.' Slowly, he drew himself upright before swinging his legs carefully over the side of the bed. With exaggerated caution, he stood, pulling himself to his full height and flexing his shoulders. I couldn't help admiring the view even though I was still embarrassed. Usually, by the time a man saw a girl first thing in the morning, it was too late; the deed had already been done. I tried not to think about what I looked like. He wandered out of the room in a T-shirt and boxer shorts, firmly closing the door behind him. I got up and glanced in the mirror. God! I opened the door marginally and peered out. John was in the kitchen and I could hear the kettle warming.

I emerged some moments later in a sweatshirt and joggers, my feet bare.

'Morning... again.'

John poured water into two mugs and turned towards me. 'Look, I'm sorry. I didn't mean to embarrass you.'

'No... You di... I just...' I blurted incoherently. 'It was just a shock, that's all,' I finally managed.

'Sorry.' He moved towards me, taking my shoulders and pulling me towards him. Once again, my head came to rest on his chest. I'd wanted him in the flat for weeks, but hadn't been prepared to end up in bed with him quite so soon. After a few moments, he took my head and turned it to face him. Bending down, he kissed me briefly on the lips. I could feel the energy surge through my body as I closed my eyes and savoured the moment. I wasn't finished, but when I opened my eyes, he was already turning away to grab a teaspoon.

We settled in the front room, John again took the armchair, leaving me disappointed on the sofa. 'You want some breakfast?' I asked.

'In a while.' He looked around the room as if noticing its details for the first time. His eyes lingered over my collection of framed prints, predominantly portraying the exaggerated beauty of young women seen through the eyes of the Pre-Raphaelites. His eyes came to rest in the corner. Balanced precariously on a small wicker chair was a pile of discoloured furry animals: bears, rabbits and a long white baby seal: relics from my childhood. 'Cute!' he exclaimed with a smile.

'Yeah, well,' I said defensively, 'you were young once too.'

Any hopes I may have had for a relaxing day with John evaporated the moment the phone rang. We both looked at it nervously. It could be the next communication from a deranged killer. Alternatively, it might just be someone wanting to talk to me. My hand trembled as I lifted the receiver.

It was Garratt. He was at work on a Sunday morning and wanted to see me ASAP. I was reluctant to leave John alone in the flat, but I figured the surveillance teams would keep him safe.

Garratt wasted no time asking me about a one thousand, eight hundred and forty-three pound charge recently incurred on my credit card.

'What!' I exclaimed.

He watched my reaction. 'I take it you didn't incur that charge?'

'No!'

He changed the subject. 'The credit card company logs and records all calls relating to fraudulent use and stolen cards. They have no record of your having made a call to cancel your card. It just seems to have been added to a list of cancellations. They've no idea who was responsible but they're producing a list of people who have access to the procedure. I understand it's going to be a pretty long list.' He shrugged. It was a start. 'Your current account now has a balance of one thousand, one hundred and sixty-eight pounds, mainly due to a credit last week of one thousand, two hundred and eleven pounds.'

I didn't need a calculator to realise that without the phantom transfer, I'd be overdrawn. 'Where from?' I asked.

'From the Metropolitan Police.'

'How come?'

He shook his head. 'It went through the same channels as your monthly pay cheque, only no-one at this end authorised it. I've advised Accounts and they're checking it out.' He paused and took a deep breath. 'Finally, there's your savings account. Or, I should say, there isn't, because it was closed three days ago, the same day your credit card was cancelled.'

My head bowed. My savings account represented all the

money I had in the world. Now it was gone.

'The balance, three thousand, one hundred and twenty-two pounds was transferred to an account in the name of Celia Potter.'

I looked up sharply. 'Celia!'

'That's right.'

'How is all this possible?'

'Well, security at banks is pretty tight. They've got their people working on exactly how it was done. They swear hackers can't get into their system, but if someone can get into the Pentagon, then no-one's absolutely secure. Anyway, that's you. The other two girls also had problems. Lucy Falkus was a trainee manager at a local supermarket, earned quite good money and was saving to buy a house. She had over eight thousand in her account shortly before her abduction. When her body was found, there were only a couple of hundred pounds left. Funny thing is, whoever transferred the money left enough to cover her existing standing orders and direct debits. So presumably, he was familiar with her transaction history. We haven't got details of where the money went yet, but she had a telephone banking account. So if someone got into her flat, as they obviously did, and they knew her passwords, they could have done it from there.'

I remained silent. 'What about Celia?'

'You already know she was having problems with her credit card. Someone made three unauthorised transactions, one of them in New York. She was a student, so she never had much money. Her bank statements indicate an average balance of less than two hundred pounds. Hand to mouth stuff. We're trawling through the transactions. There don't seem to be any that stand out as unusual, until your generous donation of three thousand pounds, of course.'

'So, what happens now?' I asked. I wanted my money back.

'We've got people from the banks checking transactions and procedures and we have a finance team here working on it. Considering the fact that someone misappropriated over a thousand pounds of *our* money, they were understandably enthusiastic.'

'But these are all different banks, right? Different credit card companies?'

'Yes.'

'So, it's unlikely a disgruntled employee could have carried out all the transfers.'

Garratt shrugged. 'Until I know more about the way the systems work, I don't know. It *seems* unlikely. From our point of view, I've got Maggie Forshaw coming in this afternoon. She's in charge of payroll for this office. She feeds the salary information to head office every month and we're all paid from there. She knows the procedure inside out. She's going to talk me through it.'

'What can I do?'

'We finally managed to track down an IT technician. He's listened to the tape from your answering machine, but the quality's not good enough to put through a computer. He's outside now.' Garratt pointed to a scruffy individual wielding a tiny screwdriver, a computer in pieces on the desk in front of him. 'He's configuring a portable for you to take back to your flat. If you can turn it on and plug it into your phone line, it'll respond when you get another call. Don't worry, there's nothing else on it. It's brand new. So, if it's infected with a virus it won't matter.'

'All right.'

'By the way, no fingerprints on the harlequin postcard.'

That came as no surprise. 'Is John okay?' he asked.

'Yeah, I wouldn't want to be in the flat alone right now.'

'No, I understand. Make sure he takes it easy. We don't want a relapse.'

I nodded.

So, I was being dangled on a line in front of an unknown perpetrator with a "Here I am. Come and get me" notice hanging round my neck. I had surveillance teams around my house and some maniac was sending me postcards and making anonymous phone calls. I also had the compensation of temporarily cohabiting with John. A local safety officer paid me a visit to check and improve my security. Having gained access to Celia's flat without breaking in, we assumed the perpetrator had managed to acquire keys to my flat as well. Consequently, we changed all my locks, just in case.

'What was Jordan Lassiter doing in Rotterdam?' Jeffries asked, throwing me with the unexpected change of direction.

'How the hell would I know?' I told him indignantly. I did know, but I wasn't about to tell him, especially since the case against Max Schneller was ongoing. He was a major Dutch drug baron, whose operations Jordan had successfully penetrated. It should have been a relatively easy bust: one Algerian courier; a suitcase full of cocaine and a whole squad of officers observing his every move. Get the picture? Somehow where Jordan was concerned nothing was ever simple.

★

When I got back to the flat that evening, John was fine: there hadn't been any more phone calls and no post. I plugged the specially prepared portable computer into my phone line. The next time I received an electronic whistle, its modem would answer.

We spent some time deciding who should sleep where. I insisted that John take the bed. He wouldn't hear of it. I was equally adamant that I was going to sleep on the couch. 'Bloody obstinate,' he called me, which for my money was a little uncalled for. We finally ended up sharing the bed. Again. The sacrifices I make for my friends! It was very chaste, no touching, not even a goodnight kiss. The pair of us lay there wide awake for about an hour, trying to pretend we weren't attracted to one another. In the end, I finally dropped off.

Hours later, when the phone rang, we both sat up sharply. I was shaking by the time the ringing stopped. John put a comforting arm around me. That was all the encouragement I needed! I must admit it was difficult: not exactly the way I'd imagined our first time would be. Whenever John adopted a different position, some part of him screamed with pain and he had to lie down again. He was very persistent, but in the end he just lay there while I did all the work. Not that I minded. I'd expected frenzy and clumsiness, passion and discomfort. What I got was docility and the distinct impression that he was only half there. It was just lucky his injured groin didn't altogether preclude normal activity.

Somehow we fell asleep in each other's arms. Looking back, I don't know quite what we were thinking. Some deranged lunatic had just left his calling card on the computer in my front room and there we were exploring each others' bodies before snuggling up together and falling asleep again. We didn't even use anything, if you know what I mean. I guess that's it: we weren't thinking at all. I was scared and clung to the nearest thing I could find for some comfort: John. I don't know what his excuse was.

So when the alarm woke us early in the morning, I climbed wearily out of bed. I remember casting a glance down my naked body to make sure that the whole episode hadn't been a dream. My lingering smirk of self-satisfaction disappeared as soon as I entered the front room.

Tick-tock, tick-tock...

When we'd gone to bed, the computer screen had been blank. Now the screen was black, except for a central pixelated rendering of a metronome. Its inverted pendulum made graceful arcs across the screen in time with the ticking. *Tick-tock, tick-tock...* And all in the same apparently deep tone, overloaded with treble by the tiny speakers. I sank to my knees in front of the table, watching the manic pendulum complete its sweeping journey from side to side. 'John!' I squawked his name for several minutes before he dragged himself up, threw on a pair of natty boxers and joined me. He stood behind me staring in mute silence at the hypnotically sweeping pendulum. 'What do we do?' I asked hopelessly.

'I guess it's some sort of screen saver, but I don't know much about it. We should probably wait for someone who knows what they're doing. We don't want to screw it up.'

'I'll ring Garratt.'

He was already on his way over. The team monitoring my calls had dragged him out of bed when they recognized the electronic signature of a modem.

We hastily threw on some clothes and made ourselves presentable. Then I spent a few moments roughing up the sheets I'd left on the sofa, trying to make it appear as though one of us had slept there. John shook his head, probably wondering why I bothered. I didn't want anyone thinking I was that easy.

Anyway, Garratt didn't seem too interested in the sleeping arrangements when he arrived. He walked straight to the computer and stared at the metronome.

'Interesting,' he muttered. 'According to our records the call was made at 5:33am?' He looked towards us for confirmation.

'About then,' John replied. I remained silent, although I could feel my cheeks flushing. I hadn't even looked at the clock. My mind had been focused elsewhere.

'Paul Bodin is on his way over.' The name meant nothing to me. 'The guy who fixed up the computer. He should be here in about fifteen minutes,' Garratt told us, looking at his watch. 'Any chance of a cup of tea?'

We discussed the situation over mugs of steaming tea. There'd been no activity reported by the surveillance team and an examination of the flat showed that the scratches on the outside of the windowpane remained the only damage. 'The next step would be for him to get inside,' Garratt remarked, familiar with the procedures employed by the perpetrator on Lucy and Celia. 'That's going to be a problem with John here twenty-four hours a day.'

'And all the locks have just been changed,' I reminded him.

'Right, but there's never been any sign of a break-in. Whoever he is, he's had access to keys. You need to be very careful,' he said, looking at me. Like I didn't already know! 'Hopefully, we'll get something from this,' he said, pointing at the computer.

Paul Bodin interrupted a protracted silence when he arrived about half an hour later, having lost his way through the back streets. 'Sorry,' he blurted, 'got lost.' He carried a heavy, reinforced briefcase, which he deposited alongside the table before kneeling in front of the computer. 'Ah!' He looked around at our expectant faces. 'Has anyone touched anything?'

'No,' came three responses.

He touched the in-built rollerball on the side of the screen and instantly, the metronome was gone. I sighed with relief as the ticking was finally silenced. Bodin opened his case and removed a thick cable and a portable disc drive. Using an extension lead, he plugged in the drive and connected it via the cable to the computer's parallel port. 'This is an exact copy of the data I put on your system, excluding the operating system itself. I'm going to compare the file lists to see what's been added.'

As he tapped away on the tiny keyboard, Garratt asked, 'Will you be able to identify the number the call was made from?'

'Yeah, hopefully, but it might not be too helpful.' Small neon lights began to flash on the computer and on the disc drive as the machines talked to each other. A dialogue box which would contain details of any discrepancies between the two file lists opened. 'This guy's obviously hacked into other systems,' he looked up at Garratt. 'He had access to the Met's payroll. He could have left behind a time-delayed procedure.' He shrugged his shoulders. 'It would automatically activate at 5:30 and transmit the files, as long as it made a connection at the other end. When was the first call?'

'Two days ago,' I replied.

'So, if he'd set it up then, he could have asked it to repeat the message every two days if there was no answer. What I mean is, he wouldn't have had to be in front of a computer last night.'

'And the computer it was sent from isn't necessarily the one he used to set it up?' asked John.

'That's right.' The computer emitted a short beep, signalling the completion of its task. 'Here you go,' Bodin said. 'Three new files.' He pointed at the screen, 'That's the screen saver, the metronome. This one's a graphic file.' He double-clicked on the file name and a graphics programme opened, the hourglass visible as the file slowly loaded.

An indistinct black and white drawing appeared. It was a picture of a dark dungeon where a native girl was hanging from a rope by her left wrist. Her right ankle was tied tightly behind her back to her right wrist, which resulted in her spine assuming a concave shape. The rope passed through a pulley mounted on the ceiling and ended at a winch, the handle of which was operated by a man lurking in the shadows to the left. He appeared to be exerting considerable effort forcing the handle further round. A guard in some kind of exotic uniform protected the door to the right of the illustration. The quality of the picture made it difficult to tell, but the girl's free left foot seemed to be dangling just inches from the floor. By stretching as far as her foot would allow, her toes could just have touched the ground and helped ease the pressure on her wrist. However, we could make out something directly beneath her foot, a sharp conical spike imbedded in the floor. Every time she put pressure on her foot, the spike would imbed itself further into her flesh.

'This is what happened to Lucy,' I said quietly, remembering her injuries.

'Jesus!' whispered Garratt.

At the foot of the illustration, towards the righthand side was a grey button reading, Caption. 'Seen enough?' Bodin asked and, without waiting for a response, clicked on the button. The screen was instantaneously filled with a representation of a white sheet of paper with small writing. The title at the top was in bold: Torture of a Native Girl in Trinidad. We were silent as we read the accompanying text:

> On February 24, 1806, Sir Thomas Picton, late governor of Trinidad, was convicted of torturing a native girl named Louisa Calderon, to extort confession. And this is the tale, gory, gruesome and cold-bloodedly inhuman, which was evolved bit by bit, during the course of the trial. In the December of 1801, the girl Calderon, then aged eleven years, was living with Pedro Ruis as his mistress. The girl, it appears, was not faithful to Ruis. She was carrying on an intrigue with one Carlos Gonzalez, who, as a friend of Ruis, frequented his house. Gonzalez, not content with robbing Ruis of his lover, took some money as well. He was arrested, and the girl Calderon, suspected of being an accomplice, was arrested with him. She denied complicity, and Sir Thomas Picton thereupon gave orders for her to be tortured.
>
> The torture itself took a rather unusual form. According to the depositions of Louisa Calderon herself, she was carried to the room where the torture was prepared. Here she was suspended by the left wrist from the ceiling, her right hand and foot were tied together behind her back, while the extremity of her left foot rested on a wooden spike fixed in the floor. In this painful position she remained for three quarters of an hour. The next day the torture

was repeated. On both occasions she swooned away before she was taken down.

Swallowing his distaste, Garratt turned hopefully to Bodin. 'Can you tell anything from this?'

He shook his head. 'No. It's been scanned from some book. Given the poor image quality, it was probably enlarged and lost some of its clarity.' He closed the graphics programme and pointed at the one remaining file on the list, called FlexTech.EXE. 'This other one's a programme and it's quite large. There's no telling what it may do. I'll take a look at it back at the office, but I want to see if anything else has changed.'

'I thought those were the only new files,' I said.

'Yes, the only *new* ones. Some of the existing files may have been changed or overwritten.'

Bodin ran another programme from the disc drive and, in a short time, it highlighted several files. 'These have all been changed.' He pointed at a specific file. 'That one could trigger his new program at a specific time. My guess is that he downloaded the files, but the computer would run okay for a few days. Then something would trigger the programme and everything would go haywire.'

'Just like Celia's,' I pointed out.

'Where did it come from?' asked Garratt.

Bodin minimised the two dialogue boxes and opened another application. 'This logs all incoming calls. There it is: 5:31am. That's the number,' he pointed and Garratt made a note. 'That's about all I can do here. If it's okay, I'll take it away and have a closer look.'

It was clear from his eyes that our engineer, Paul Bodin, was scared. He was an IT technician and wasn't used to getting so close to the action. Although he was in no personal danger, he'd recognised the tension in the air. I was convinced then that he would stop at nothing to help us. His subsequent actions proved my point beyond anything that I could possibly have imagined.

Bodin and Garratt departed and left us staring into space, trying not to think about what had happened.

Chapter 7

All the above I recounted to Jeffries. Yes, I know he'd asked about Jordan, but previously he'd asked about the phone calls. If he was going to hear my story, he'd hear it my way, in my own time. I was trying to recount events in a vaguely chronological order, despite the variety of his prompting. Jordan wouldn't be drawn into the case for another couple of days. She'd drop everything in response to my frantic phone call. Within hours, she'd wish she'd stayed in Rotterdam.

'Tell me about Nadia,' Jeffries suggested.

Whoa! That was *some* change of subject. Here I was, recounting details of the case, telling the truth for a change, and he wanted me to stop and jump to events after that night in the safe house. Nadia, I should explain, was Jordan's adoptive mother, and wouldn't make her debut in the story for some time yet. Due to an unfortunate combination of events, I would never actually meet Nadia face to face. That was something I genuinely regretted. She was Jordan's only surviving relative and had brought her up after her parents' unfortunate demise. I didn't want to think that far ahead.

So John and I spent the day together, busily thinking of things to take our minds off my problems. We didn't have to think too hard. Despite his frail condition, we spent several hours in the bedroom, 'cementing our relationship'. If we hadn't been so occupied satisfying our carnal desires, we might have noticed a strange man watching the flat from the foot of the garden. Despite the surveillance team logging everyone who entered or came out of a neighbouring alleyway, his presence wouldn't draw anyone's attention until the following day. Bringing a dog with him was a nice touch. What could be more natural than an old man walking the dog on a sunny afternoon? Needless to say, the team stationed at the rear saw absolutely nothing. The general consensus of opinion was that the man hadn't approached the flat because he saw I had company, but maybe he had just been on a scouting mission. We'd find out the next day.

On Tuesday morning I reported for work as normal and was immediately summoned to DI Garratt's office. I nodded a greeting to Bodin, who was also present, and took a seat next to the computer. He glanced up at me with a look of concern and I smiled to assure him I was okay. Without saying anything, he double-clicked an icon and suddenly a familiar scenario played out. The lettering shuddered and individual characters dropped down the screen until they were all assembled in a black bar along the base. Next, the screen turned black and a grief-stricken angel phased into view, joined seconds later by her halo. Then, as if floating on an unseen cloud, she scrolled right and the word 'Martyr' appeared. Soon, the words turned blood red and dripped into a sickly pool. I'd hoped never to see it again, and the memory of it turned me icy cold.

'It's exactly the same programme as the one we found on Celia's machine,' Bodin explained. 'Different name, but the same programme.'

'What about her machine?' I asked. 'She kept a diary of incidents.'

Garratt passed me a printed sheet, on which I quickly recognized the first three entries. The complete list read:

Telephone calls started, silent
Harlequin postcard
Changed telephone number
Telephone calls again, silent and computer generated
Window scratched – outside
Changed locks
Strange smells
Car scratched
Window scratched – inside
Computer virus?
TV scratched
Clothes bleached

I noted the absence of the dissected mouse, although its presence could have explained the 'strange smells' entry. In the space of a little more than three weeks, Celia's life had been turned upside down. The final unwritten entry should have read '*abducted*'. It would have been dated just four days after the bleaching incident. The list was interesting, but was of little help. A log of the iniquities that had befallen her after her abduction would have been more useful, but we would be left to piece that together when we found her body, if we ever did.

Remembering the name of the file that included the *Martyr* program, I asked, 'Any idea what FlexTech means?'

'They're a company based in Macclesfield, but they have offices all over the country,' answered Bodin. 'They employ computer technicians and hire 'em out to anyone who wants them. They write software, correct problems and help specify and install new systems. They do everything really.'

'How many people do they employ?' I asked.

'About seven hundred at the last count. They're preparing a list of everyone who's worked for them in the last five years, but it'll amount to thousands. It's a very flexible business. If they hire someone out and their new employers like the look of him, they often poach him. But there's a good chance that they once employed our man. Maybe he still works for them. It's about the best thing we have to go on right now.'

'Have they ever been employed here?' I asked tentatively.

Unfortunately, the answer to that question was 'Yes'.

I was sent packing to the collator's office: a small room I'd seen altogether too much of since I started working for the police. Whenever anything interesting was happening, stakeouts, raids or confrontations with armed thugs, Ramsden consigned me to the collator's role. I found it insulting but I guess he thought me a bit frail to confront violence. Very soon I'd be forced to confront much, much worse.

The call came at 11:06 am.

I'd been pottering about not doing anything very constructive, my mind ranging from Lucy's injuries to the logistics of Saint Cecelia's broiling. I made endless cups of tea I didn't really want until I noticed the sell-by date on the box had expired several months before. Then I switched to coffee and the increased levels of caffeine made me even more nervous and jumpy.

Then I received an urgent call from Linda, Inspector Garratt's secretary. She instructed me to meet him immediately in the car park.

'Why? What's happening?' I asked, trying to keep the fear from my voice.

'DI Garratt will explain everything. He's waiting for you,' she said tersely.

I flew down the corridors and up a flight of steps. In the car park, Garratt stood beside an imposing navy-blue saloon, leaning on the open door. I dashed over the crumbling concrete. My face was flushed as I approached the car. I called out, 'What's going on?'

Garratt sat in the car and pulled his door closed. Throwing open the passenger door, he explained, 'There's been some activity at your flat.' He started the engine and looking back over his shoulder reversed out of the space.

'What's happened?' I pressed.

'Someone set a fire outside the window.'

'They caught him?'

He hesitated as we pulled onto the street. 'No.'

I sighed in frustration. 'How come?'

'I don't know the details. We'll find out when we get there.'

I could hear reluctance in his voice, as if he was holding something back. Then, quietly I asked, 'What about John?'

Garratt looked both ways as he pulled out into a busy junction. 'John's back in hospital.'

'What!?' I cried.

He shook his head. 'That's all I know.'

Garratt's claim to ignorance didn't stop me asking endless questions about different aspects of the morning's events. He responded patiently but, by the time we drew up outside my flat, his patience was wearing pretty thin. Two squad cars were parked at an angle to the kerb on either side of the entrance and several uniformed officers stood in the street chatting with two men in civilian clothes. A couple of bystanders holding plastic shopping bags stared from a distance and opposite the house, several watching faces were visible behind their windows.

We got out of the car. I followed Garratt as he pulled aside the two plain clothes CID officers. 'What the hell happened?' he demanded.

The two officers looked at each other, unsure where to begin. 'I was at the back,' admitted the shorter of the two. 'Someone got into the garden. He must have come through the other gardens from the alley.'

'Didn't you see him?' asked Garratt incredulously.

'No!' He replied sullenly. 'He must have crawled along beside the fence. I didn't know anything was wrong until I saw John charging down the garden.'

'He did what?' I asked in horror.

'He came charging down the garden screaming. Something was on fire underneath the bedroom window. He may have seen something.'

'He's supposed to be resting,' I insisted.

The officer shrugged.

'How come we didn't see this guy coming out of the alley?' asked Garratt.

The officer who had so far remained silent, looked up sheepishly. 'I think I did. I *must* have. There was this old guy with a dog. He was the only one to come out of the alley at about the right time.'

'Why didn't you pick him up?' I asked.

'I didn't know anything was wrong until Phil got on the radio! By the time I got down there, he'd long gone.'

Garratt shook his head in frustration. 'So, then what?'

'We both came down the alley from different directions. It was empty, no-one there.'

'So where was John?' I cried.

'We found him in the garden next door. I don't know what happened. He was unconscious. They took him away in an ambulance.'

Terrific! We'd both known the dangers of a relapse if John overexerted himself. I should never have suggested he stay at the flat. I didn't think anything would happen while we were surrounded by two surveillance teams, but we were in the process of discovering that their vantage point at the rear of the house was hopelessly inadequate. Nobody knew John's current condition. He could have had another confrontation. He could have been battered over the head with an iron bar, again.

While I concentrated on John, Garratt continued a heated exchange with the two officers. I shrank away in shock as Garratt put his hand on my shoulder. 'We need you to take a look around,' he informed me.

'No!' I replied sharply. 'I need to get to the hospital.'

He took his time, before asking me to follow him to his car. Leaning through the open door, he picked up the radio and asked to be connected to PC Sutter, who had accompanied John to the hospital. After a short delay, Sutter's voice came across the airwaves, 'Sir?'

'What's PC Wilson's condition?' Garratt asked tersely.

'They've taken him down to X-ray.'

'What do the doctors reckon?'

'He took another blow on the head. They're not saying anything until they've seen the X-rays.'

'Okay. Let me know when there's any news.'

It was futile and we both knew it. If I went to the hospital, I'd only be hanging around for hours while they diagnosed his latest injuries. So I took a look around the flat. Nothing had changed, except for an accumulation of soot on one of the windows. I stepped outside, where scene of crime officers were already examining the remains at the base of the dustbin. Light bulbs flashed, impressions of footprints in the soil were being taken and the bin and window frame dusted for prints.

I could see some scorched remnants in the bin: colourful and textured, like a knitted jumper. As I watched, a white boiler-suited officer slotted an object into a clear evidence bag and passed it to Garratt. He held it up for me to take a look. Inside was a piece of jewellery, a pendant on a silver chain. The pendant was unusual. It looked like an upturned miniature urn or an inverted minaret, with a hint of eastern design. 'It was Celia's,' I said calmly, handing it back.

'Are you sure?'

I sighed. Police officers were supposed to be observant. Maybe when you attained the rank of Inspector you left such things to your minions. 'She was wearing it in the photo,' I pointed out.

'Which photo?'

'On the 'Missing' poster.'

'Oh, right!'

'Presumably that's what's left of her clothes,' I mumbled studying the charred remnants. 'Now all we need is the body,' I added and walked back inside.

So John was back in hospital, and Jordan… Jordan was in Rotterdam on the trail of this individual by the name of Schneller. He was one of the untouchables, having established a network of organised crime covering the entire continent. Recently, a number of personnel successfully planted at various levels throughout his organisation had gone missing.

They never found their bodies but Jordan managed to piece together a detailed summary of their last known activities. What did she do? She had a little tête-à-tête with Max Schneller over a cup of herbal tea in a Rotterdam coffeehouse. It wouldn't be the last time we heard his name.

Meanwhile Lawrence Arnold was presumably very happy with the situation at my flat, because he was about to step up his campaign. Soon, we'd discover exactly what he'd done to Celia. It wasn't pretty.

'Can I have some tea?' I asked Jeffries.

He sighed and walked to the door, instructing someone to rustle up some refreshments. When he sat back down, he told me, 'You're not being very helpful.'

So I explained how further examination had shown that the initial phone calls to my flat had been made from the local police station, as had been the calls to Celia's flat. Bodin tried to give us a crash course in modern technology, but his efforts were largely wasted on me. I gathered that it was possible to piggy-back calls via several switchboards and have an incorrect number logged as the caller. I expect the perpetrator thought he was being very cute using the station as his bogus number, leaving us floundering. All that was about to change.

After Bodin identified the *Martyr* program on my computer, named FlexTech, Garratt got onto the company and told them what was going on. He demanded they tighten their security and render all current passwords obsolete. Initially, they refused point blank, but he insisted, threatening them with a court order. It was a real pain for them because it meant that all seven hundred employees would have to be issued new identities and passwords: an administrative nightmare. However, Garratt hoped that by severing any potential gateway to FlexTech's sophisticated system, he'd be preventing Arnold from gaining access. It was a hunch. There was no evidence that Arnold was using their system, but by selecting the company name, he was pointing a finger in their direction. And sometimes hunches paid off.

I was still shaking by the time I arrived at the hospital, frantic with worry. I'd heard no further bulletins about John and had endured a bad-tempered debriefing session with Garratt and the two surveillance teams. There was just a sliver of hope remaining. All those entering or leaving the alleyway had been photographed and logged. The films were rushed to the lab for developing. Hopefully, we'd caught the bastard on film.

I arrived at the hospital not knowing whether John was alive or dead. At that very moment, the emergency doctors could be pummelling his chest in an effort to restart his heart. Tubes could be attached to his arms, feeding life-preserving fluids into his system, while his face was covered with an oxygen mask. Okay, maybe that was a bit pessimistic, but he had a fractured skull and there was no way of knowing.

I flew along the corridors, reaching A&E where I was referred to a small cubicle. When I burst in, John was lying there casually chatting to a uniformed WPC. They both looked up startled. I must have looked a right spectacle, breathless, open-mouthed and sweating.

'Can you give us a minute?' John asked the WPC.

'Sure. I'll be outside.' She stood and departed through

the curtain.

I looked at him, silently cursing him and everyone else for not letting me know he was okay. His head was back in a thick bandage. It looked like he was wearing a stunted turban. The flesh around his left eye was puckering in preparation for an impressive shiner. But he was smiling, smiling at me. 'Are you all right?' he asked, concerned by my appearance.

Was I all right! I moved wearily to the chair but instead of sitting down, I threw my arms around his shoulders and rested my head on his chest, looking away from him. The sight of him conscious and smiling was more than I'd hoped. I couldn't help crying.

'Hey!' He took hold of my head and attempted to turn it to face him. I shook my head firmly. I wasn't about to let him see me crying. 'Come on,' he urged and I gave in. The face I presented to him was bright red, though I was slowly regaining control. I was panting a bit, but my composure was almost back. My cheeks were still damp with tears and he reached across to the trolley, took hold of a white towel and tenderly wiped my face dry. 'I'm all right,' he assured me.

I collapsed in the chair. I leaned forward, my elbows on the edge of the bed. I gave one final sniff and wiped my face again with the towel. 'I thought…'

'I was dead?' he suggested. 'I'm fine. Apart from a headache.'

'What happened?'

'Someone was in the garden.'

'I know that! What happened to you?'

'Oh!' he said, sounding embarrassed. 'I chased him down the garden. He'd cut a hole through the wire fence, so

I followed him. I was crossing the garden next door when something hit me.' He stopped abruptly.

'What? Did he...?'

'No. It wasn't him. I could see him ahead of me. He'd almost made it to the alley by then.'

'So what was it?'

'I have a feeling it was probably the branch of a tree,' he said slowly.

'What!?'

'Yeah.' He swallowed. 'I have a nasty feeling I ran into a tree.'

I said nothing. It was better that way. 'You weren't supposed to go outside,' I reminded him accusingly. 'No exertion. That's what the doctor said.'

'What was I supposed to do? Just watch him get away?'

'Yes! That's exactly what the surveillance teams did! You could have been killed.' I attempted to look angry, but I couldn't hold the expression. My relief was too great. 'Christ! What's your mother going to say?'

'We'll soon know. She's on her way.'

'Oh, God!'

I sensibly made myself scarce before his mother arrived.

It had already been quite a day, and unfortunately, it wasn't over yet. It was still early afternoon and the excitement had barely begun to run its course. They were keeping John in overnight at the hospital for observation, and I wasn't about to stay alone at the flat. That night I'd retreat to the section house again. Events later that night would remain at the forefront of the police force's memory for a long, long time.

On my return to the station, I was hustled into Garratt's

office where he was explaining the complete and utter failure of the surveillance teams to a senior officer who looked seriously unimpressed. I'd only just sat down when a WPC burst in. 'What!' barked Garratt impatiently.

'Sorry, sir. I think you should come and look at this.' She darted back out of the door and we rose obediently to follow her.

As we entered the main office, every face was turned towards one of the many computer screens. We pushed through a crowd in front of the nearest one. The screen was blank, except for a central murky black and white illustration, showing some sort of scene with a fire raging in the background. The details were difficult to pick out, but as I craned my neck and studied the image more closely, I began to feel nauseous. Five men in extraordinary costumes, with huge plumes coming out of their helmets, stood around a central table on which a person was tied down, face upwards. They looked like court jesters with their hats and baggy trousers, but they weren't laughing. Situated on the tethered person's body, covering their genitals, was some kind of circular container on top of which a fire had been ignited. Flames shot up towards the ceiling as the figure lay apparently unconcerned, hopefully unconscious.

I took hold of the mouse and clicked the familiar button labelled, *Caption*. Remembering the previous text I'd forced myself to read, concerning the agonies of Louisa Calderon, I hesitated, but as the pictorial sheet of paper was delivered to the screen, I knew I'd have to read it. The title read: *Torture of the Rats*. I felt sick before I started.

> *One of the most revolting, and at the same time most unique methods of torture was that used at one time in Holland. The victim was stripped, and tied hand and foot, face upwards, on top of a table or bench, or secured to stakes fixed in the ground. An iron vessel, or basin-like shape, containing several large doormice or rats, was turned upside down upon the prisoner's stomach. The next step was to light a fire on top of the metal container. The animals, driven frantic by the heat, and unable to escape, burrowed their way into the prisoner's entrails.*

'Jesus!' whispered Garratt as I paled. We were both aware that if our perpetrator was true to form, Celia would have been forced to undergo this torture, just as Lucy Falkus had been forced to relive the agony of Louisa Calderon. I couldn't begin to imagine the horror.

'I don't understand,' said Garratt, looking around for someone who would meet his gaze. 'Where did this come from?' As he looked around the office, he confirmed that the same illustration was present on every monitor.

There was silence.

'Well, how did it get on the machines?'

'I've no idea,' volunteered some brave soul, 'but we can't get rid of it.'

'What?'

He walked to the terminal where we stood and proceeded to stamp as many keys as he could with one hand. Nothing happened. 'It's completely dead. All we can do is flip between the picture and the caption. Nothing else works.'

'Get someone from IT up here. Now!' Garratt shouted and retreated to his office.

I stood very still, abandoned as shocked officers wandered around not knowing what to do. I heard the call being made to IT, but couldn't shake the vision of Celia Potter strapped to a table with demented rats boring into her body. Suddenly, it was more than I could stomach and with my hand clutched to my mouth, I raced from the room, reaching the toilets just in time to deposit what was left of my breakfast in a sink.

A girl called Siobhan was swiftly despatched to check I was okay. She received strict instructions from Garratt: 'Stay with her! Don't leave her alone. Not for a second!'

When I returned to the office, Garratt was nowhere to be seen. While I was waiting, I sat at an unoccupied desk and reached for the phone. Siobhan sat opposite. 'Can you give me a minute?' I asked. She nodded and retreated an extra yard. I shook my head and punched in a set of numbers from a scrap of paper.

'Yes,' came the surly response.

Relieved that she'd answered, I said simply, 'It's Allison. I need your help.'

There was a pause. In the background I could hear birds singing. 'I'm leaving for Beijing in the morning.'

'Oh!' I groaned.

'What do you need?' Jordan asked.

'Protection,' I replied quietly. 'Someone's trying to kill me.'

There was an even longer pause. 'What's going on?'

'You know what happened to Celia Potter and Lucy Falkus?'

'I picked up a few things.'

'Well, now it's happening to me. The same!'

Jordan sighed. 'Why didn't you tell me?'

'I don't know. I thought...'
'Where are you?'
'Castleton nick.'
'Stay there. It's going to take me some time.'
'Where are you?'
'Rotterdam.'
I groaned again. I'd hoped she was back in the country.
'Don't worry. I can be there in a few hours.'
'What about Beijing?' I asked.
'Beijing will wait.'

So there it was. When I eventually managed to get in touch with her, I just snapped my fingers and she came running. It really was as simple as that. I sat back and awaited her arrival.

Chapter 8

When Garratt returned, I was ushered into his office and Siobhan dismissed. She closed the door as she left. I couldn't even bring myself to look at him. I sat staring at the blank wall in front of me, nibbling my fingernails.

'I've just been with the Deputy Chief Constable,' he started. 'He's authorised twenty-four hour protection for you. There'll be two bodyguards, twelve hour shifts. You're to stay in the section house unless you hear to the contrary. They'll make quite sure you do.'

'What about John?' I asked.

'There's a man on his door at the hospital. When he gets out, he'll stay in the section house as well. We'll have people on the doors and people inside. You'll both be quite safe.'

I looked down at the table. 'Jordan's coming,' I muttered.

'What!'

'Sergeant Ramsden told me she was the best bodyguard on the force. Well,' I paused. 'That's what I want.'

'She's suspended. She won't be allowed in the building.'

'Well, if she can't come in, I'll have to go out, won't I?' Okay, so by this time I'd been reduced to the level of a petulant schoolgirl. But that was the way I felt.

'Allison, she's a disaster waiting to happen!' It came as quite a shock when I found out Garratt was right: Jordan's presence wouldn't help alleviate my problems; they'd make matters considerably worse. He sat back with a long sigh. 'Look, we know all about your budding friendship with Jordan. When she started poking around asking for post-mortem photos, we put a marker on the file.'

I swallowed guiltily and looked up. 'I gave them to her,' I admitted.

'I know. Perhaps you could tell me why.'

I took some time to consider my answer. 'The dead girl was involved in her case.'

Garratt shook his head. 'That's pure speculation.'

It was my turn to shake my head. 'No, it's not! I've seen the evidence.'

Garratt spent a while analysing my features before massaging his temples. 'Then why hasn't she brought it in?'

I shrugged, 'Maybe because she's suspended and you won't allow her in the building.'

After a lengthy sigh, he went on to detail the strategy being employed to identify our killer. They'd received a lengthy list of all current and past employees of FlexTech and were attempting to match the names to individuals who had worked at the Met. The killer had gained access to the force's payroll and credited me with over one thousand pounds. Clearly, he was familiar with our systems. Over-familiar, you might think. They were also trying to tie the list back to people who'd worked with Celia or Lucy on the off-chance that the killer had known them personally. It was a daunting task. There were thousands of names. The combined legwork of the entire Metropolitan Police would have taken weeks to narrow the list of suspects.

As a result of Garratt's hunch it would prove unnecessary. Because FlexTech had disabled all their security protocols, Arnold couldn't gain access to their system. Given time, he could have re-established a gateway, but time was a commodity he was running short of. He was a genius on the computer. He could have hacked into anyone's system, but he didn't need to. While he was working on various assignments, he established hidden paths through which he could gain remote access. Once inside, he could send his little messages in complete anonymity.

However, as one doorway closed, others remained wide open. Denying him access to FlexTech's system proved crucial. As a direct result, we would finally identify him. We would also locate his most recent lair. What we didn't know was that one of those wide open doorways, swaying gently in the breeze, would enable him to access the most confidential information of the Metropolitan Police. If we'd known that, we would all have been scared.

'Tell me about finding Celia,' Jeffries suggested, once we were suitably refreshed.

There are certain incidents during the course of events that I tried very hard not to think about. Finding Celia's body was one. The night at the section house was another. Then there was our stay at the safe house. Oh yes, and what I'd later discover in a left luggage locker at Paddington station...

Events were moving quickly now. While I sat around waiting for Jordan's arrival, Paul Bodin was working to trace the number from which the *Torture of the Rats* picture had been transmitted. After a couple of frustrating hours in the canteen, I was summoned to Garratt's office again.

A news blackout was in operation. Even so, experienced journalists could smell a story miles away and had begun toying with theories. Details of the torture and humiliation endured by the victims had so far remained confidential. Somehow, one of the more serious broadsheets had obtained a copy of the painting of Saint Cecelia from the Rijksmuseum, the same one I'd received on a postcard. They intended to print a story the following morning and had forwarded a draft inviting a police response.

When I arrived in Garratt's office, the sheet was sitting on his desk. Immediately, I recognised Saint Cecelia, but alongside her was another picture. A young girl in a full-length red dress and black shawl stood in the middle of a flaming pyre. The flames had yet to ignite her clothing, and her face bore the same high forehead and contented tranquillity as Saint Cecelia. Three individuals, partly cut off by the borders of the picture, carried large leather bellows to fan the flames. Another figure on the right, apparently running towards the girl, carried a long sword and, with a lunge, had embedded its point deep into her throat. It didn't take a genius to figure that the picture portrayed an image of Saint Lucy.

'It's from the *Master of the Deposition from the Cross of Figdor*,' Garratt explained. 'Whatever that is! A detail entitled the 'Legend of Saint Lucy'. It's also in the Rijksmuseum in Amsterdam.'

'Where did they get it?' I asked, wondering why we hadn't received a copy ourselves. It was unnerving to think that the media were better informed than we were.

'Both illustrations were sent anonymously to their crime desk. My guess is that Celia received a copy. Anyway, one of their reporters put it together, tied it to Lucy Falkus and guessed the connection to Celia.' He sighed. 'They're going to be all over this tomorrow.' He rubbed his eyes before continuing slowly. 'Have a seat, there's a few other things I need to tell you.'

There was some good news for a change. The bank had

acknowledged the fraudulent transactions on my account and agreed to rectify the problem. Everything would be exactly as it had been before. I'd still be overdrawn, but at least I'd have my savings back.

'Take a look at these,' Garratt requested, handing me three blow-ups of photos. 'This is the guy we think set the fire in your garden. Someone's taken copies to the hospital so John can confirm it.'

I looked at three blurred prints of a dark figure in a voluminous windcheater and flat cap. A bustling Jack Russell pulled on a lead from his outstretched arm. The man's face was indistinct but appeared to have a thick bushy moustache flecked with grey. Where the eyes should have revealed more, his sockets were bathed in dark shadow, his head slightly lowered. His neck was concealed with a scarf. Over his shoulder was a strap and I could just make out a bag hanging on his back.

'Any ideas?' asked Garratt hopefully.

'Stalin?' I suggested.

'I assume you don't recognise him.'

'Is this the best we can do? Can't they be enhanced?'

'They *are* enhanced.'

I shook my head and tossed the photos back on the desk.

'What about him?' he asked, passing me another two photos.

This time I was looking at a thin, taller man in a full-length raincoat. Again he had a dog, this time a more imposing and better behaved Labrador. A floppy trilby covered the man's head. The picture was of better quality and I couldn't fail to miss the man's thick black beard and horn-rimmed spectacles. Again, a bag's strap was wound over his shoulder and this time it was more visible. 'Who is this?' I asked, shaking my head.

'We think it's the same man. We have him logged entering the alley yesterday afternoon, but he never made it through to the other end. He came back out the same end nine minutes later.'

'This bag,' I said pointing at the photo. 'It could be Celia's. It looks like the one I wore during the reconstruction.'

'That would make sense. It's obviously full here,' he said, pointing to its bulging contours. He picked up one of the photos of the Stalin lookalike. 'It looks empty here. So, he carried Celia's clothes in it the previous day, but didn't set the fire. He came back the following day to do it.'

'Why?'

'I don't know. Maybe because there were two of you in there on Sunday: more chance of being spotted.'

'Did you get anything from the clothing?'

'Fibres and hair, possibly saliva. It'll be important when we find the guy. There's probably enough to confirm his identity.'

'Probably?'

'Well, we won't know until we catch him.'

There was a knock at the door and the face of Paul Bodin appeared. 'We've got the number!' he exclaimed.

Garratt took a moment to catch his thoughts. 'The number the virus was sent from?'

'Well, technically it isn't a virus, it was a programme called FlexTech. We'd received those lists from them yesterday, so someone must have run it and...' He left the rest blank. The result was all too obvious.

'What's the number?' Garratt demanded, grabbing a

pencil.

'It's a house right here in town,' Bodin said excitedly and passed Garratt a slip of paper with the details.

Garratt leapt to his feet and went out into the office. 'Listen up everyone!' he shouted, clapping his hands. 'We have an address from which the last message was transmitted: 14 Engadene Street. The current owner is a Mr Andrew Thompson.' He turned to DS Cochran, a designated team leader. 'Put together a team to take the place apart. I want uniforms, I want dogs and I want the enforcer,' he added, referring to the weighted, metal battering ram they used to break down stubborn doors. 'And I want to be ready to move in half an hour!'

Chapter 9

That was our first break, and all because Arnold hadn't been able to piggyback the call via FlexTech's system to hide his location. An uneasy thought was still nagging at the back of my mind: he was a computer genius and he'd already shown us that he could use multiple false numbers. Why hadn't he? *The Torture of the Rats* file had led us straight to this location. Why? The only answer I could come up with was that he wanted us to find the house. He'd left something for us but he wouldn't be there.

The house's owner, Andrew Thompson, was run through the computer. He'd been dead fourteen years.

Forty minutes later a sizeable task force had assembled and squad cars blocked both ends of Engadene Street. It was a long, narrow road with trees planted into the pavements at regular intervals. The kerbs were packed with parked cars and it was a gloomy neighbourhood. The houses were terraced and identical to one another: two storeys with gabled roofs.

I hung back beside the roadblock with Garratt, observing from the back seat. He hadn't wanted me to come, but I'd insisted. I figured I was safer with them than on my own at the station. He made me promise that no matter what happened, I remained within his sight at all times. A contingent of officers in thick protective clothing was advancing on number 14 from both directions. They took up position crouching behind a short brick wall that marked the extent of the front yard. A stairwell led downwards to a stout basement door. When they entered the house, officers would attempt a simultaneous entry to the cellar.

Garratt's radio hissed as one detachment reported that they were in position. Several others followed swiftly, confirming their readiness. Uniformed officers were stationed in the back garden. Other officers blocked the adjoining street, in case the occupant attempted to flee through the rear.

I watched as Garratt raised the radio to his lips, depressing a black button. 'Go! Go! Go!' he shouted, and immediately there was noise. I could see the troops rushing the front door and announcing themselves. They stood to one side allowing access to the enforcer and seconds later an almighty crash accompanied the door being smashed open, the frame around the locks shattered. Shouting all the while to disorientate any occupants, they made their way inside as Garratt awaited news over the radio. I could picture officers charging up the stairs and bursting into the upper floor rooms.

After several minutes, the radio burst into life. 'All clear in the house!'

More loud crashes rang out as they continued trying to gain entry to the basement. Several bewildered neighbours had appeared and were swiftly instructed to get back inside. 'Come on,' Garratt instructed, holding open the car door. 'Stay with me.'

We marched down the street, ignoring the commotion on either side as officers attempted to coax unwilling householders back inside their properties. The basement door resisted all efforts to break it down and, as we approached, the disgruntled officers were making their way back up the stairs. 'Must be reinforced,' mumbled one with a shrug of his shoulders.

Inside the house everything was reasonably neat, although the interior could have done with a good clean. In the kitchen, dishes and plates stood on a draining rack and a soiled mug contained evidence of a morning cup of tea. Nobody touched anything, knowing fingerprints could be important. The house would later be turned over to a forensic team who would search for traces of the occupant and of Celia, assuming she'd ever been there. A brightly coloured shoulder bag sat by itself on the kitchen table. 'It's Celia's,' I said in a low voice.

I heard footsteps echoing off the floorboards upstairs but my attention was focused below. There had to be access to the basement. Then I understood: the shoulder bag was a signpost. I donned a pair of latex gloves and took hold of one end of the kitchen table. 'Give me a hand,' I urged Garratt. Together we moved the surprisingly lightweight table to one side. I bent down and pulled back the rug: too delicate for a kitchen. Any spilled liquid would permanently stain its pale pigments. Hidden beneath it was a trap door and a terrible rancid smell was escaping from around the frame. I stumbled backwards, nearly losing my balance, holding my hand over my mouth.

Garratt turned to DS Cochran, who selected three officers to descend into the basement. They produced powerful torches and indicated they were ready. Cochran threw open the trap door and attempted to ignore the sickening smell. Garratt and I waited in the safety of the kitchen as Cochran shone the torch's beam downwards and revealed a short passage. At its end was the door the officers had failed to break down. He looked up at his colleagues. 'There's two rooms off a central passage. You two take the right. You,

you're with me on the left. Okay?'

Swiftly but hardly silently, the four men descended the bare wooden stairs, taking up position on either side of the two doors. We watched the beams of torchlight criss-cross the darkness. On an unseen signal from Cochran, the two doors were thrown open. For a moment there was complete silence. Then I caught sight of something small darting from the room on the left. It was only momentarily illuminated by the beam of a torch, but soon a light switch was thrown and several more creatures appeared. I groaned. I'd hoped the illustration of the *Torture of the Rats* was a warning, an unreal menace culled from the sick pages of history. As I saw the furry long-tailed rodents scuttling in search of cover, I knew it was more than a threat. It had come true for Celia Potter.

The two men emerged from the left-hand room visibly shaken. 'I think you'd better get down here,' suggested Cochran.

Garratt started to descend, taking shallow breaths against the overpowering stench. 'Stay here,' he instructed, but I followed hard on his heels.

As we approached ground level, we could hear the squeaking of the terrified rats and the patter of their tiny feet as they sought shelter beneath the stairs. I took a deep breath and stepped onto the tiled floor. I wished I'd had some bicycle clips, but fortunately the rats were occupied elsewhere and ignored me. 'Do something about these rats!' Garratt ordered no-one in particular as he approached the door. He strode straight in. During his many years on the force he had seen death assume all manner of guises, but even he was brought up in his tracks by the spectacle facing him.

His bulk blocked the door, reluctant to venture closer. I

had to push him aside and squeeze through the doorway. My mind registered different pieces of equipment in the room, but I ignored them all, concentrating on the sight of what had once been Celia Potter. Her naked body lay on a long table, her battered arms and legs tightly tethered by leather restraints. On her abdomen rested an inverted metal pot, like a large cast iron casserole. Its uppermost surface bore traces of the fire that had burned on its surface, driving the rats into a frenzy of burrowing. The sides of her torso had been ripped open where they'd finally tunnelled free. Surmounting the ashes atop the pot, staring straight towards us in open-eyed resignation, was Celia's severed head.

Contrary to all my expectations, I felt strangely detached. There was no sense of horror or panic. I saw exactly what I'd prepared myself for. Celia Potter's suffering was over, ended in a particularly horrific manner. It was our task to ensure that the perpetrator was caught before anyone else was forced to endure similar torment. I moved forward, leaving an entourage camped beside the door. I bent and examined Celia's neck. Trailing leaves of flesh dangled like petals from a dying flower. Her neck bore two distinct and deep lacerations, fulfilling Saint Cecelia's prophecy: three times they had attempted to cut off her head. The flesh on her torso was discoloured and blistered: Celia had been 'broiled' alive. Only an post-mortem would reveal which of her injuries proved fatal.

I turned away from the corpse and noticed the pulley on the ceiling, through which the rope that suspended Lucy Falkus had run. In the floor below was an empty circular recess. While Lucy hung from her wrist, the hole had contained a vicious spike that bored its way through her flesh and into the bone of her foot. A crudely constructed, robust wooden winch stood abandoned in a corner. The handle had been turned and Lucy had risen and fallen depending on his perverted fantasy. Hanging on the wall on either side of the door were two pictures. They weren't framed: just prints pinned to the plaster. They were larger versions of the paintings of Saint Cecelia and Lucy.

'There should be a sword,' I commented to no-one in particular.

Against his better judgement, Garratt took a step towards me, using his bunched handkerchief as a mask. 'Sword?'

'There has to be something he used to cut off her head.' I scanned the room again but couldn't see any suitable weapon.

I'd seen enough. I turned and walked past the stunned men, crossed the corridor and entered the opposite room. The room appeared to have been a workshop with a wooden bench, vice and sundry woodworking tools. It had been left surprisingly tidy, but its smell shocked me: the room smelled of newly cut wood. My mind went back to the discomfort of the reconstruction. My overwhelming memory as things began to go hazy, had been the smell. Now I recognised it as freshly cut wood.

No wood shavings or chippings littered the floor and a bulging black plastic sack rested against the wall. The room contained little of interest: there were no half-completed contraptions he could later employ on other unfortunate victims and no sword. I imagined he would be devastated at being forced to abandon his lair. Or perhaps not. He knew enough not to have had to use his own phone number. It could only mean that he had been ready to move on. But why, and to where?

And that's exactly what I recounted to Jeffries. I even told him the bit about calling Jordan.

In moments of personal stress, I can still picture Celia staring wide-eyed at me from atop a cast iron pot. At that stage, I didn't know in which order her injuries had been inflicted, whether the rats had shredded her flesh before or after she was dead. The thought was too much to contemplate. Delayed reaction, they call it. Garratt and I were understandably subdued as we drove back to the station. Subdued that is until I screamed at him to stop. After an admirable emergency stop, I deposited my latest sandwich in the gutter in front of countless shoppers outside Woolworths. I didn't think Jeffries needed to know that.

'That night you stayed at the section house,' Jeffries continued.

'Yes.'

'Tell me about it.'

So I did: as comprehensively as I could, although much of it has been lost forever.

When we arrived back at the station, Garratt reported to various senior officers and I was allocated a uniform to babysit me. When he returned he told me tersely, 'Everything's ready. You'd better get to the section house.'

I looked up with a frown. 'Jordan's not here yet.'

'She's on her way up.'

'Oh! You decided to let her in?'

He smiled. 'Yes. I want a word with her before you go.'

Suddenly, the office was overcome by an unnatural hush.

I glanced through the open door and saw all heads facing in one direction. They gradually turned as the object of their scrutiny moved through the office. Then she was standing in the doorway. 'Come in,' Garratt told her. I don't know why he said that. She was already in.

In contrast to the stern ponytail she'd sported on our previous meetings, Jordan's hair was loose and flowed along behind her, flicking her shoulders as she crossed the office. The effect was dynamic, her loose hair softening the sharp contours of her face and framing it with a gentle blonde halo, imbuing her with a sense of femininity I hadn't previously thought possible. Wayward strands stubbornly clung to her cheeks and she coaxed them back into position with her fingertips. Her large eyes peered out from behind golden wisps and somehow she didn't seem as menacing. She looked pretty, like she belonged on the cover of a magazine. She glanced at me, concerned. 'You all right?'

'Yeah,' I mumbled, still absorbing the drastic transformation.

Jordan looked around the room twitching her nose, before focussing back on me. 'You still smell of vomit.'

I sighed. Jordan had a remarkably sensitive nose. 'We found Celia's body.'

Jordan nodded. She looked at Garratt but he averted his eyes. 'Shall we go?' she asked me.

'Jordan,' Garratt started. 'We need to talk.'

She looked at him sternly. 'What was it you told me last week? "I have neither the time nor the inclination."'

'Jordan!'

They stared at each other for some time as if they were lifelong enemies, but I knew it wasn't like that. They were both just intransigent, not an ideal arrangement for mutual co-operation. 'Allison,' said Garratt. 'Can you give us a minute?'

Before I had a chance to stand, Jordan instructed sharply, 'Stay!'

'Jordan, I understand you're withholding evidence.'

She looked accusingly at me. I tried not to look guilty. 'So, suspend me!' she suggested. Then she returned her attention to me. 'Let's go.'

I looked at Garratt who shrugged in resignation. He'd dealt with Jordan often enough in the past to know that he wouldn't get any information out of her until she was good and ready.

I felt self-conscious as four people surrounded me for the short walk to the section house. That wasn't counting Jordan, who brought up the rear, casting her eyes in every direction. It took about ten minutes to negotiate security on the door, a fact from which I drew some comfort. We were allocated a room and closed the door in an attempt to block out the rest of the world. It was a single room with few amenities. Bathrooms and kitchen were shared and located at each end of the narrow hallway. There was a single bed, chair, desk, wardrobe and not much else. We both knew what to expect having occupied similar rooms during training.

It was apparent as soon as she locked the door that Jordan was uneasy. She drew the curtains and refused to sit down. I perched on the bed and tried without success to coax her into a chair. 'Thanks for coming,' I told her.

'No problem.'

'What's the matter?' I asked as Jordan continued prowling.

'Nothing,' she replied as if her mind was elsewhere.

'Jordan!'

She took a deep breath. 'This isn't the way I work. I haven't secured the perimeters; I haven't vetted the occupants; I haven't searched the building for weapons; I haven't prioritised potential areas of vulnerability. I don't even know how many entrances there are!'

'It's all been taken care of,' I told her.

She shook her head. 'That's not how I work.'

'Will you relax? You're making me nervous.'

With a sigh, Jordan sat in the chair. I couldn't help noticing she didn't sit back, but perched on the edge of the seat, ready to spring at a moment's notice. 'Tell me about Celia.'

I grimaced. I didn't want to remember. Reluctantly, I began to recount the events of the day, culminating in the horrors of Engadene Street. Jordan listened intently throughout, remaining quiet and allowing me to narrate at my own pace. I wrapped up the tale by adding, 'Her injuries were consistent with what we know about Saint Cecelia: her skin was red and blistered and her neck had been cut three times.'

Jordan reflected for a moment. 'How did he broil her?'

'What?'

'I can understand how it was done in Roman times: in a hypocaust. How would you do it in a domestic basement?' Her forehead creased as she worked through the problem.

'Jordan, I'm not interested in the logistics.'

She looked at me accusingly. 'You should be. Details are important.' She mused for some time before commenting almost appreciatively, 'He's very thorough.'

'Jordan! That's what he wants to do to me!'

'Don't worry,' she said, her mind elsewhere.

'Don't worry!'

'I won't let him.'

I looked up at her, smiling. There was no-one I would rather have had with me; her confidence was infectious. 'You know, you're not at all what I expected,' I told her.

'No?'

'No. You're supposed to be some sort of ogre.'

'Disappointed?'

'No!'

Jordan relaxed marginally, her shoulders releasing their tension. 'I told you, I'm just selective. I choose my friends carefully.'

'You hardly know me,' I pointed out.

'I know you better than you think.'

'You do?'

'I made it my business to find out,' she told me.

'Like what?' I asked warily.

'Well, I know you were once disciplined for urinating in the school fish pond.'

'How did you know that?' I demanded, spluttering.

'I like to know what I'm getting myself into.'

'I was six!'

'The fish didn't know that,' she remarked casually.

'The fish survived!'

'What about the carp they found floating on the surface next morning?'

'How...?'

'Tinsel, wasn't it called?'

I took a deep breath. 'He died of old age.'

Jordan shrugged.

'Is this how you go about striking up a lasting friendship?'

Jordan eyed me seriously. 'I have to be careful.'

'Why?'

'I've made a lot of enemies.'

'I wonder how?'

There were times when I didn't appreciate Jordan's close attention, like when I placed a call to John in hospital. Jordan refused to leave my side, even when I went to the toilet. At least she was prepared to wait outside the cubicle. Though she insisted on checking it first just in case a masked gunman was concealed in the cistern.

A few minutes later, she was relaxed enough to open the evening paper and skim the contents. I was toying with a book, not really reading, unable to concentrate. As she turned a page, her whole posture stiffened. Staring back from a grainy photo was someone she hoped she'd never see again. 'Shit,' she muttered.

'What's up?'

'Someone I used to know,' she remarked enigmatically.

I couldn't get anything more out of her. She was like that. Her brain was calculating the damage she could be subjected to, incorporating the new facts. Later, when she'd completed her mental arithmetic, she'd tell me. The article in question concerned the release from prison of a man named Raymond Ives. He was the small-time thief who'd been apprehended with the proceeds of his latest burglary still on his person. Along with her partner Tamsin, Jordan had been instrumental in putting him away. Now that he was free, he would launch a high profile campaign to reopen the investigation into the death of his girlfriend. It was an incident Jordan understandably didn't wish to relive.

She fidgeted incessantly. Twice I attempted to attract her attention when her mind was clearly elsewhere. I appreciated the speed with which she'd detached herself from whatever she was involved with in Rotterdam and come rushing to my side, but I figured she had some unfinished business there. She kept looking at her watch and mumbling inaudibly. Then her mobile phone chirruped. She barked a familiar response and then listened in silence for some time. 'No!' she told someone sharply, 'I can't.' She listened again before remarking, 'I have something on.' She said very little but I got the impression that whoever was calling was pretty agitated.

'Problem?' I asked once she had terminated the call.

She shrugged. 'Rotterdam.'

'What about it?'

'There's been a hitch.'

'Should you be there?'

She shrugged again. Conversation closed. I'd later learn that initially the operation in Rotterdam was an unqualified success. Working on information Jordan had 'coerced' from a Turkish go-between, Dutch police had intercepted a courier and recovered an unusually large consignment of cocaine, leaving one notorious drug dealer very unhappy. Unfortunately, while we were occupied in the search for Lawrence Arnold, the whole operation would turn pear-shaped and the recriminations would start. Jordan wasn't the sort of person who passed unnoticed in a crowd. It wouldn't be long before her presence in Rotterdam was common knowledge. Dealers aren't generally very nice people. They tend to hold grudges.

Even a condemned man is allowed a phone call. It took

a lot of persuasion, but Jordan eventually let me use her mobile to check up on John's progress. Still in hospital, he was feeling a lot better, despite a lingering headache. The doctors seemed satisfied and had stated their intention to release him the following day, assuming his vital statistics remained within tolerances. I told him about our new instructions and he swore, not relishing the prospect of being confined to the section house. Not only that, we would each be allocated single rooms. He didn't think much of that either. I thought he had enough to worry about, so I didn't tell him about Jordan.

A young PC was despatched to my flat to collect clothes, food and anything else I thought I might need, including my small portable television. I thought it might make the hours pass a little faster. Closeted in our room, Jordan sat in the only armchair, tuning the television as I unpacked. She watched the screen with a frown, as if the programmes were in a foreign language. I looked at Jordan as she fiddled with the controls. There was something about her: something impossible to define. When I finished allocating my clothes to drawers and hanging up the few items that required hanging, I turned my attention to a plastic bag of groceries. 'I'm hungry,' I said, but failed to elicit anything more than a grunt from Jordan. 'I'm going to the kitchen.'

Jordan leapt to her feet and in a single lithe movement knocked a glass ashtray off the coffee table. Fortunately it landed on a rug and didn't break. She picked it up effortlessly, and placed it with exaggerated care precisely at the centre of the table. 'Wait,' she ordered and, stooping slightly to avoid banging her head on the frame, went through the door.

Each floor had its own kitchen at one end with bathrooms at the other. The lockers were housed in a sub-basement. In the days of sexual segregation, each floor had been single sex. A monitor used to be positioned at each stairway to ensure propriety. Now, any available room was allocated on a first-come first-served basis, with only the bathrooms retaining their original designation. We were on the first floor and were lucky enough to have a female bathroom at the end of our corridor.

'It's empty,' whispered Jordan, returning from the kitchen.

I didn't care if it was empty. I would have welcomed a conversation with a colleague. 'Are you eating?' I asked Jordan.

'Yes.'

I rifled through the bag looking for something that didn't take a lot of preparation. There wasn't a lot there. 'You like chilli?' I asked finding two microwave chilli con carnes.

'What's in it?' she enquired.

'I don't know.'

'Okay,' replied Jordan, turning up her nose in distaste.

I was fast learning that Jordan wasn't a great conversationalist. I considered telling her what my mother had told me when I was younger, 'You're not properly dressed without a smile', but I thought better of it.

Jordan didn't stop looking around, as if expecting someone to leap out and knife me. It all seemed ridiculous until I remembered those faded illustrations and thought of the last few days in the life of Celia Potter.

We made it to the kitchen without incident and without meeting another soul. An occasional television set was audible behind closed doors, but no-one ventured into the corridor. I stabbed a few holes in the plastic containers, shoved them in the microwave and searched for a couple of decent plates. Jordan put on the kettle and extracted a purple sachet from her pocket, depositing it in a cup. I opted for tea.

'What the hell is that?' I asked, pointing at the sachet.

'Ginseng and blackcurrant,' she replied curtly.

As we waited patiently for the kettle to boil and the clock on the microwave to tick down, I thought about instigating a conversation. Jordan amused herself by rearranging the cutlery and crockery until everything was perfectly aligned. Then she turned her attention to the fridge, relocating bottles on the shelf so that the tallest was on the left nearest the hinges and the shortest on the right. I watched in silence. The kettle boiled and she poured water into the two mugs. A few minutes later, Jordan whisked the liquid with a teaspoon and extracted the sachet. 'Try it,' she suggested.

Turning up my nose, I took a small sip of the liquid. 'That's disgusting!'

Jordan nodded. 'It grows on you.'

'Yeah, like fungus.'

Before the microwave finished its cycle, the calm of the section house was shattered by an alarm bell of terrifying volume. 'Jesus!' I screamed, blocking my ears with my hands. About two feet from Jordan's head, an old-fashioned red alarm bell was ringing. Jordan didn't flinch and, reaching into her pocket, extracted another purple sachet and carefully inserted it between the bell and the clapper. The deafening noise was greatly reduced, but shards of purple vegetation started escaping from holes in the sachet. 'It's the fire alarm,' I stated rather unnecessarily.

Jordan made no reply and gave no indication of impending movement. She was obviously deeply troubled.

'We're supposed to assemble in the car park,' I informed her.

'Right,' she said reluctantly, her hand reaching into her pocket for what I expected was a concealed weapon.

Jordan led the way, pushing rudely past my colleagues who turned angrily towards her, before withdrawing silently. In the lobby, she conferred with the guard at the door. They drew me between them and watched as people in various stages of disarray streamed past us into the chilly evening.

'Shouldn't we be...' I pointed to the door. I felt distinctly uncomfortable flagrantly disobeying regulations.

'Stay where you are,' I was ordered above the continuous ringing.

Every floor had a reluctant safety officer, each of whom bore a clipboard with a list of current residents. They were the last out of the building, having checked toilets and bathrooms. In the car park outside, roll calls were being made to ensure everyone was accounted for. Within minutes, the wail of fire engines could be heared, followed by their flashing lights as they drew closer. The lobby lit up in red and blue as they pulled to a halt beside the front doors. A fire fighter in heavy-duty kit burst through the doors. 'Why the hell are you still inside?' he demanded.

Jordan pulled herself to her full height and confronted him, moving uncomfortably close and towering above him. Her biceps bulged from her stretched T-shirt as she explained, 'We're staying inside.'

He considered the situation for a few seconds before backing down: the tone of her voice didn't encourage dissent. 'Where's the control panel?' he asked and was led away by one of the safety officers.

'Jerk!' remarked Jordan and sat back down on the reception desk. It bowed slightly beneath her.

Minutes later the building was given the all clear. A smoker had triggered the alarm in the toilets on the third floor. The troops began to file back and Jordan insisted on checking every name against a central register. She denied admittance to police officers who had every right to be there, and to visiting friends and colleagues unless they were on the register. A great deal of moaning ensued and several friends, or maybe ex-friends, glared at me before turning away into the night. Jordan's presence ensured the matter didn't get out of hand.

When everybody was safely accounted for, Jordan left her colleague to man the front door and escorted me back to the kitchen. When we arrived, two girls, one of whom I recognised, were making cups of cocoa. When they saw Jordan, they spluttered, 'We were just going.'

They grabbed their mugs and walked away, leaving a tempting aroma of cocoa behind them. As they hurried past, I was too embarrassed to make eye contact. 'Sorry,' I mumbled.

I shook my head and turned to Jordan. 'You have a talent for emptying rooms.'

'It's a gift.'

Silently, Jordan opened the microwave and withdrew the containers. They were still warm. She pressed the lever on the pedal bin with her foot and prepared to drop them inside.

'What are you doing?' I asked.

'We can't eat this.'

'Why not?'

'Someone may have tampered with it.'

'Jesus, Jordan! You've got to stop reading those cheap thrillers!' I took a deep breath. Maybe enlisting Jordan's help had been a mistake. 'I'm hungry and I don't have anything else to eat.' I grabbed the two containers and thrust them back in the microwave. I turned the dial to four minutes and returned my attention to the kettle to make a fresh cup of tea.

We made it back to our room without further incident. The microwaved heat of the chilli was enough to incinerate my mouth on contact, but Jordan didn't seem to notice and finished hers while I was still picking at the edges. It was the only occasion I ever knew her to eat food stuffed full of E-numbers. She must have been famished. She'd pretty soon learn it was a big mistake. She sat patiently, flicking the channels on the TV until I finished. She seemed to derive little pleasure from the purple liquid she was drinking, grimacing every time she took a mouthful.

'I have to go to the toilet,' I told her.

'Fine! Get ready for bed.'

'It's only nine o'clock!'

'It'll save us having to make another journey.'

'I might want to go to the toilet again.'

'You should learn to control your bladder.'

I had no doubt Jordan rigidly controlled every functioning part of her anatomy with precision. We encountered another girl in the bathroom. 'It's all right,' I assured Jordan before she had a chance to throw the girl out.

Despite the early hour, I felt unusually drowsy when I returned to the room. Jordan took her place in the armchair, having secured the door behind us, and I remember thinking how odd she looked when she yawned. The action seemed so totally out of character. She was the very epitome of efficiency in everything she did, but now she looked as though she was struggling to stay awake. My eyelids were similarly heavy as I began to undress. By the time I reached my underwear, Jordan was motionless, her eyes tight shut. *Odd!* I thought as I picked up my T-shirt. Suddenly, I didn't have the energy to remove what was left of my clothing. Half lying, half falling, I sprawled onto the bed. I was unconscious before my head hit the blankets.

So there we were: two upstanding members of the police force, unconscious and entirely at the mercy of a deranged lunatic. But there were guards stationed at the doors checking everyone's identity, vetting every occupant. The premises had been searched and I had two armed bodyguards, only one of whom was currently sleeping like a baby. We should have been completely safe.

Chapter 10

Everything was hazy.

The bright light hurt my eyes.

My vision was blurred.

My mouth was dry and the foul taste was indescribable.

I had a momentary feeling of complete disorientation. Then I moved my head marginally to examine my surroundings.

The section house!

I felt better having identified my location. I was safe at the section house. I was alive! That was the main thing, or so I thought. Then the events of the previous day came flooding back, along with a memory of the sight of Celia's severed head, and my stomach responded uneasily.

Sunlight streamed through the billowing curtains. It must be time to get up, I thought, turning my head to where I expected to see my alarm clock. A thousand jackhammers started to pound in my head and very gently, I lay back on the pillow. I screwed up my eyes and tried to take shallow breaths, but the pain made me gasp.

Jordan!

I suddenly remembered her and looked towards the armchair, careful to move my head as little as possible. She was still sitting there, but she was completely naked, her arms draped casually on either side. 'Wow!' I muttered as I took in her physique. Her muscles bulged in places I didn't realise I had muscles. She was almost completely flat chested. Huge wads of gracefully curving muscle dropped down from her shoulders and consumed her breasts. A pair of rosy red nipples jutting out from the surrounding plateau of her chest were the only indication that I was looking at a woman. Just to make certain, I took a glance further down, below her washboard stomach. I didn't see any body hair. I mean none! Of course, that could have been a matter of personal choice, but I couldn't help wondering whether it was.

I raised my eyebrows. She certainly wasn't at her best. Sleeping, I couldn't see those eyes, and her mouth hung open, snoring contentedly. She's probably a lesbian, I thought uncharitably, but I didn't remember her being bald.

She's bald!

That *did* strike me as odd. I tried to recall the previous evening, but my memories stopped abruptly at the fire drill. I was fairly certain she had hair the previous evening. I could remember admiring it: a mass of blonde hair framing her face. I screwed up my eyes in confusion.

Then the absurdity of the situation finally struck me as the random pieces began to fall into place. Jordan had assumed the duties of my bodyguard and I could remember her performing them with awesome professionalism. Now here she was, stark naked, asleep in an armchair. And she was bald!

Something was seriously wrong.

I looked down the length of the bed in which I was lying. The covers were pulled up to my chin, respectably covering my body. I lifted them up and looked underneath. I was naked too. I didn't usually sleep naked.

'God!' I exclaimed, reaching for my head, thinking the unthinkable. I breathed a long sigh of relief as my hands tangled in my hair. I wasn't bald! The sudden movement threatened to split my head apart. I fought the pain and forced myself upright, holding the covers in place below my chin. 'Jordan!' I croaked. There was no response.

I swung my legs over the side of the bed and attempted to locate my clothes. They were neatly stacked on the side table. I couldn't remember doing that. The room smelled like spicy foreign food and beside the door, I noticed two empty plates. I stood unsteadily and reached for my clothes.

With great difficulty, I pulled on my underwear. I was unsteady on my feet, propping myself against anything within reaching distance. I crossed the room to Jordan and gently shook her shoulder, trying to rouse her. It took a while, but she finally opened her eyes. After the initial sight of me standing there in my underwear, she quickly closed them again. I shook her harder. This time her eyes quickly flitted onto her own body slumped in the chair. Judging by her facial expression, her head hurt almost as much as mine.

'Why am I naked?' she growled accusingly and stood abruptly, pushing me backwards. She grabbed my shoulder for support as she fought to remain upright on her trembling legs. She stood leaning on me with her head bowed. Slowly, her right hand went to where people usually kept their pubic hair. 'What...?'

That answers that question, I thought, trying not to grin. Despite the seriousness of the situation, I felt incredibly lightheaded. It was all I could do not to burst out laughing. I considered breaking the news to her gently, but eventually with a sigh, I took her other hand and lifted it to her head. She collapsed back down into the chair. 'Not again,' she mumbled quietly. 'I don't understand.'

'Neither do I,' I responded. 'We need some help. Get dressed,' I told her.

★

Most of the morning passed in mute silence. I suppose we were both in shock, but the more Jordan recovered, the more red-faced and angry she got. I remember lying back in an examination cubicle at the local hospital, my head still spinning, watching as she paced up and down. She was driving me mad. We were safe and that was all I cared about, but Jordan was far from happy. If you looked closely, you could see several small cuts where a razor had nicked her scalp.

'Jordan, why don't you sit down? You're making my head spin.'

She managed to convey a definite hint of malice in her ensuing snort. She refused to look at me.

As she skirted the bed, I laid a sympathetic hand on her arm. She pulled away sharply as if stung by a wasp.

'Jordan,' I repeated quietly.

'What?' she replied aggressively.

'Sit down.' I stretched out my hand, but Jordan ignored it.

'Why?'

'Because I want you to.'

She considered my request for a few moments before emitting a long sigh and wearily taking a seat next to the bed. Her eyes focused in her lap and if I didn't know better, I would have sworn she was planning some hideous vengeance. As I watched the red mist envelop her eyes, I could imagine what was going through her mind.

'It wasn't your fault,' I reassured her. 'You warned me.' Without raising her head, she finally met my eyes. My blood turned icy but I wasn't about to let it drop. 'We weren't prepared.'

'It's my job to be prepared!'

I took a deep breath and tried a change of subject. My mother always taught me to offer comfort to animals in distress. 'How old are you, Jordan?'

She looked up confused. 'What?'

'How old are you?'

'Twenty-six.'

I smiled. 'You've done pretty well for yourself.'

She stared ahead blankly.

'You're a woman of few words,' I suggested.

She shrugged.

'What do you do for relaxation?' I asked, and watched her face cloud over.

With a slight shake of the head, she answered, 'Gym, shooting range, swimming.'

'Nothing else?'

She shrugged.

'You don't like the cinema or eating out?'

'Sometimes,' she answered rudely.

'What do you do with your friends?'

'Friends?' she asked.

'Your *carefully selected* friends,' I reminded her.

'Nothing.'

'Oh,' I responded quietly.

'Why are you asking?'

'Hey, you're my bodyguard. I should know something about you.'

'Not any more.'

'What?'

'I'm not your bodyguard any more.'

'Why not?'

Jordan rolled her eyes in frustration and I wondered why

she made it so difficult for anyone to reach out to her. 'Because you could have been killed.'

'But I wasn't.'

'No, but you wouldn't feel safe with me, not after last night.'

I thought about my options. Jordan had been humiliated and was clearly crushed by the experience. She wasn't accustomed to failure. From now on she would certainly be on her toes. Besides, I was actually growing to like her. 'I wouldn't feel safe *without* you,' I told her.

Jordan looked as though she was working through a conundrum. She looked up twice as though ready to speak before changing her mind. 'I don't understand.'

'I want you on my side. I feel comfortable with you. Hell, we don't have any secrets from each other!'

Jordan looked like she wanted to smile. She remained silent.

'Maybe when this is all over, we could go somewhere,' I suggested.

'Together?' She sounded surprised. Maybe it was horror.

'Yeah.'

Jordan fell back into silence as she considered the idea. She wasn't used to socialising, but just this once, maybe she would make an effort.

John interrupted our conversation by appearing from behind the curtain. He was already in hospital, so when he heard the news, he rushed down two flights of stairs to see me. 'What the hell happ...?' He broke off abruptly as he noticed the tall figure sitting unusually upright in the chair beside the bed. 'Good God! Jordan Lassiter!' he stammered open mouthed. 'Who moved your stone?'

Jordan muttered something under her breath.

'You do something to upset your hairdresser?' he asked.

She snorted with contempt.

'John! It happened last night,' I explained.

He continued to focus on Jordan. 'What the hell are you doing here, Jordan? I thought you were undergoing another psychiatric evaluation.'

I cringed and Jordan's face turned dark. '*Counselling!*' she corrected loudly. 'I was offered *counselling.*'

'What about the Chinese guy? Was he offered counselling? "How to survive with no balls?"'

'I've no idea,' Jordan responded sourly. 'If he needs help, maybe you could volunteer.'

I could feel a distinct tension in the air. 'You two know each other,' I pointed out.

'Oh yes!' replied John with a smile. 'Jordan was my partner.'

'You're kidding!' I exclaimed, looking directly towards Jordan's scowling face.

'Yeah,' replied John. 'Five whole days.' He puffed out his cheeks at the memory. 'I've never told so many lies in my life as I did that week.' He shook his head. 'So what exactly's going on here?'

'I wish I knew,' I replied.

John spent an extra few seconds studying Jordan before turning to me and pulling a face. He made the mistake of glancing at Jordan again and shied away from the withering glare he received. 'So what happened?'

I shook my head, relieved that the painkillers had started to work. 'We're not too sure. We were drugged.'

'How?'

'In our chilli con carne.'

'How'd he manage that?'

I looked down, feeling guilty. 'There was a fire alarm while we were heating it up. We never went outside but I guess someone got to the chilli.'

'Tut, tut, Jordan. You're slipping!'

'It wasn't Jordan's fault. It was mine.'

'Then what?' John asked.

'That's the worrying part. We don't know. We woke up this morning and couldn't remember anything. We don't know what he did.'

'We know some of the things he did,' corrected Jordan in an angry whisper.

'You haven't been...?' he asked.

I assumed he was thinking along the lines of sexual assault, so I shook my head again, 'No.'

'So how'd he get in if security was so tight?'

'I've no idea. Garratt's looking into it.' John perched on the edge of the bed and took my hand. Jordan snorted in derision. 'You heard about Celia?' I asked.

'Yeah.'

'You wouldn't believe what she went through.'

'Yes, I would. I've had it all explained in graphic detail. So what happens now?'

'We wait here until someone comes and collects us. They're searching the section house for anything that might help. You never know, they might find something,' I said hopefully.

'They might find my hair,' responded Jordan bitterly.

★

She wouldn't have long to wait before her missing hair came to light.

Jordan was the most positive, self-assured person I'd ever met. She had total confidence in her ability to achieve anything she set her mind to. Our abject surrender that evening had left her shaken and demoralised. I don't know whether she'd ever tasted failure before, but Arnold would make sure we both became familiar with the sensation.

The hospital informed us that we'd been subjected to a powerful barbiturate. We were discharged despite lingering headaches and mild dehydration. John was also discharged. When we arrived back at the station we were summoned to Garratt's office, where he and the Chief Inspector were waiting. I'd never met the dour Chief Inspector before. I knew him by reputation. Everybody knew better than to mess him about.

The three of us took seats around a table, Jordan sulking a considerable distance from the rest of us. Garratt opened the conversation, staring accusingly at her. 'Would somebody care to explain? Jordan?'

She returned his stare with interest.

'It wasn't her fault,' I explained. 'She told me right from the start we weren't secure. I ignored her. Then she told me not to eat the chilli. I convinced her it would be okay.' I looked at Jordan, who still wasn't making eye contact. 'Next time I'll listen, okay?'

Jordan didn't respond.

After a pause, Garratt took up the reins. 'We found three cigarette butts in a room on the third floor.'

'The right brand?' I asked.

'Consistent with those found outside your flat and Celia's.'

John looked puzzled. He knew nothing about any cigarette butts.

'So how did he get out? How did he get past the man at the door?' I asked.

Garratt opened his mouth to say something, then stopped himself. 'We know the name he used: Stephen Hopkins. He was an employee of FlexTech and worked here for three months in the summer. We got his *real* name from fingerprints at the house in Engadene Street. He's called Lawrence Arnold, and he's known to the police. Anyway, Stephen Hopkins was listed as one of those staying at the section house last night. All he had to do was identify himself and walk straight past the man on the door.'

'How'd that happen?' I wanted to know.

'Every day a list is compiled on the computer. There are only so many rooms, so different people can dip in and out and allocate a room when they need one. Each afternoon, a list for that night is passed to the doorman. What we should have realised is that anything stored on one of our computers is vulnerable. He must have got access and added his name.'

Welcome to the security and confidentiality of the Met! I shook my head as the full enormity of our escape hit me. Jordan wore a mask of disgust. 'So why didn't he do anything to me?' I asked.

'I can only assume he prefers his victims to go through a prolonged preparation. A swift death is definitely not his speciality. And don't forget Celia,' he added. 'She received photos of herself, remember?'

I didn't need the reminder. I remembered Celia's closed eyes in the photo. 'Great!' I muttered miserably.

'You said this guy has a record. For what?' asked John.

'Ah! It's rather an unsavoury tale. Apparently he was in seminary training for holy orders. There was a bit of a scandal with one of the young cleaners. She accused him of attempted rape. He was never convicted but I think the chief priests took a pretty dim view of having police crawling all over the place and he was thrown out. This was up in Cumbria somewhere. They're digging out the details and sending them down.'

'What about the girl? Is it worth talking to her?' I asked.

'It was nearly thirty years ago!'

I shrugged. 'So what's he been doing since?'

Garratt shook his head, presumably wondering the same thing. Slowly, our eyes focused on the Chief Inspector. He grimaced briefly before telling us, 'We're working on it!'

'Family? Friends?' demanded Jordan.

'We're on it,' he assured us.

'Telephone records?'

'We'll have them,' he replied confidently.

'I'd love to know what really happened at the seminary,' I pointed out. 'It has to be important.'

'I've got someone trying to identify anyone who was with him,' he explained patiently.

'Do we have *any* idea where this guy could be?' asked John optimistically.

'No, but we do have his identity photo from FlexTech.' He passed us a sheet containing a colour copy of a mug shot.

He looked so normal, unremarkable in every way. A small weasel of a man you wouldn't think twice about if you met him at a bus stop. But there was something familiar... *Oh boy!* I sat up sharply. 'I know this guy,' I told them, tapping the photo with my fingernail.

All eyes fixed on me. I tried not to shrivel.

'You do?'

'Yes.' I tried desperately to cast my mind back. 'He was working in the office here. I didn't recognise the name... He was working on the collator's system while I was doing a rotation.'

'When was this?'

I tried to cast my mind back. 'Three, four months ago.'

'How well did you know him?' asked Garratt cautiously.

'I must have shared an office with him for about a fortnight. We talked, but I didn't really get to know him.' Then I remembered something else. 'He asked me out!'

'What?' asked John.

'Yeah! He asked me out for a meal.'

'What did you say?'

'I declined.'

'Politely?' Garratt queried.

'Very.'

'You didn't do anything that would have upset him?' asked Garratt.

'Apart from saying no? No... Yes!' I quickly corrected myself. 'Maybe... Oh God!' I exclaimed as an embarrassing incident came flooding back. 'It was after I finished in the collator's office. I went down there for something and Cathy was in there. Stephen wasn't there...' I thought back desperately trying to recall the train of events. 'Cathy and I got talking. She told me Stephen had asked her out and I told her that he'd tried it on with me too. She turned him down as well and we got talking about him, how creepy he was and how uncomfortable he made us feel just being in the office.'

'Why? What did he do?' Garratt demanded.

'Nothing. He didn't have to *do* anything. It was just... Sometimes a man makes you feel uncomfortable, like you're not safe. It wasn't anything he said or did. It was just a feeling. The way he stood, his whole demeanour... I don't know. There was just something about him.' They all looked blank. I sighed. 'Maybe you have to be a woman.' We all looked at Jordan, the only other woman present, but somehow I couldn't see her feeling uncomfortable in the same position. I shivered as I remembered him and then shivered again when I realised that I'd been completely at his mercy the previous night. 'Anyway, we were having a bit of a laugh about him and he walks in. I don't know how much he heard but I was glad I could walk away. Cathy had to stay and work with him.'

'You said things that would have offended him?' asked Garratt.

I lowered my head. 'Yeah.'

'Did you speak to Cathy about it again?'

'No.'

There was silence as everyone considered the situation. Then I was struck by a thought. 'You know, if we were uncomfortable with him in the middle of a police station, he may have freaked out others. You should check whether there were any complaints about him.'

'Good idea,' Garratt responded. 'I'll get someone onto it.'

We wouldn't know until our involvement in the case was over, but FlexTech had received at least one other complaint about Lawrence Arnold. He'd worked at a company in Brighton, in an office with a single mother named Denise. She'd complained about harassment to her boss, who in turn passed it onto FlexTech. They'd acted commendably fast and replaced him with another technician. However, by then the damage had been done. Several months after the case was concluded, the remains of Denise and her young son were discovered.

'What do we do now?' asked John.

'You go back to the section house.' Garratt turned away from a disgruntled John and faced me. 'You stay right where you are. I've sent a WPC round to your flat to pick up some clothes. Then we're going to put you somewhere no-one will find you.'

'Where?' I asked.

'The fewer people who know that the better. I've a fair idea, but I need to run it through the correct channels. Everything has to be watertight. We've screwed up once too often.'

'Covering your arse?' Jordan enquired.

'Call it what you like. We have to play this one by the book. Arnold's got to you once, let's not give him another opportunity.'

'Wait!' said John. 'If Allison's going somewhere, I want to go with her.'

'I...' Garratt started before being interrupted by Jordan's stifled laughter. Silencing her with a single glance, he went on, 'I don't think that's a good idea.'

John turned to Jordan. 'I'd have thought you'd appreciate an extra pair of hands.'

Jordan eyed him with contempt. 'Depends whose arms they're attached to.'

'I can help protect her!' he suggested.

'You can't even protect yourself!' Jordan responded, eyeing his vivid bruising. 'And this is no fourteen-year-old girl we're up against.'

'She was sixteen!' he spat.

Jordan sat back and crossed her arms, managing to transform a normally defensive gesture into overtly hostile body language.

Before either of them had the chance to say anything else, Garratt held up his hand. 'Enough!' He turned to me. 'What do you think?'

I weighed up my options. By this time, I was reasonably comfortable with Jordan. I was as relaxed as anyone could be with her, but her taciturn style would hardly make the hours fly past. We could be cooped up for days, weeks even. 'I guess I'd like John to be there,' I muttered, hoping I wouldn't regret it.

Jordan exhaled with such ferocity that Garratt had to clamp his hand down on his papers to prevent them from being blown away. He ignored her disgusted expression. 'Let me think about it. It's not going to be today. We have to get things ready. So you have time to change your mind. In the meantime, go to the canteen and get some food inside you.'

'What about tonight?' I asked.

'Tonight you're staying right here: in the custody suite,' he replied with a grin of satisfaction.

Jordan was having trouble controlling her disgust. 'In a cell?'

'They're very comfortable,' he assured us.

'How would you know?' she continued.

'Can't we just go home?' I asked pathetically.

'No!' he stated bluntly. 'I've had to withdraw the surveillance teams. We needed the manpower back here.'

'I...' I started. I didn't really know what to say.

'It's just a matter of time before we find him,' Garratt assured us.

'Or he finds us,' I responded quietly.

He held his hands out appealing to us. 'It'll just be one night. Besides, hot food, running water, comfortable bed...'

'Locked doors,' Jordan interrupted.

'In your case, that would probably be safest for all of us. Listen, if it makes you feel better, I'll let you keep your shoelaces.' He walked off laughing, leaving the three of us less than amused.

At length, Jordan stood. 'It makes sense,' she admitted. 'Let's get something to eat.'

Chapter 11

Following our late lunch, we made a pretty subdued trio as we wandered down to the locker room to pick up a few essentials. We'd made progress: we finally knew the name of the person we were dealing with and we'd 'captured' his London base. Of course, Arnold had pretty much surrendered the house in Engadene Street, but we were still one step forward. The forensic team was working on the samples taken from the house. Celia's body had been found there and they were looking to tie in Lucy Falkus and other, as yet unidentified, victims. They'd recovered a wealth of trace material and several sets of fingerprints.

As you might expect, Jordan was even more tight-lipped than usual. Internally, she was seething. After the previous night's events, she probably hadn't expected to be with us, despite my assurances at the hospital. Garratt had had certain reservations, but I'd insisted she accompany us. I wasn't quite so sure about my decision to include John. On reflection, I think I requested he come along purely because of our newly consummated relationship. If I was going to be in hiding for any length of time, we'd be able to take it a few steps further. Before long, he'd be quite unnecessarily exposed to danger as a result of my request. It remains my greatest regret.

Jordan insisted we stay together, not wanting to let either of us out of her sight. John extracted a few items of casual clothing from his locker, stuffing them untidily into a blue holdall. Jordan shook her head. Even after a long day, there was no evidence of creases on her outfit. I raised my eyebrows when I saw the pictures taped to the inside of John's locker door. Evidently, he was attracted to women with exceedingly large breasts. I felt a pang of disappointment.

'They were here when I came!' he explained, attempting to sound innocent. I maintained a dignified silence.

We crossed the corridor to the ladies locker room. Mine was towards the rear. I extracted the key from a bunch and slipped it in the lock. The inside was not as I left it.

Someone had been there.

As the door opened, John stared at a colour picture of himself taped to the door. It was his turn to raise his eyebrows, but I hadn't even noticed it. I was picking up a large shoebox from a high level shelf. It hadn't been there the last time I opened the locker. Jordan held it while I removed the lid. The contents solved the mystery of Jordan's missing hair. I took a deep breath and awaited her fury.

Jordan growled loudly, running her fingers through the long golden strands with a pained reverence. I could sense her becoming increasingly enraged and placed a comforting hand on her shoulder. She was breathing heavily and was evidently having trouble controlling herself. I noticed John take a small step backwards, attempting to maintain a discreet distance. I closed the box, passed it to John and took hold of both Jordan's shoulders. Her whole body shuddered and I felt the unnatural firmness of her flesh. As suddenly as it had started, the tension seemed to abate. With a deep breath, she hauled herself upright.

Concealed behind the shoebox was another, smaller cardboard box. It almost looked like a jewellery box. It brought back memories of the dead, dissected rodent I'd found in the linen chest at Celia's flat. As I picked it up, I could feel something else. Taking the box in my left hand, I reached up with my right and found a photograph. I saw myself stretched out on the bed. My arms pointed to the corners of the bed and so too did my feet. The photo was taken from the foot of the bed and despite the poor quality, it was pretty explicit, like something out of a pornographic magazine. My breathing faltered.

'What?' asked John.

I shook my head sharply and thrust the degrading photo into a pocket.

'Snap!' said Jordan as she found a similar photo nestling beneath her hair in the shoebox. She flashed it quickly at me. It was taken before her head was shaved. 'This is what I used to look like!' she informed John angrily, shoving the photo in front of his face for a second.

I don't think he had time to register anything other than her posture. From where the picture was taken, her head was furthest away. Besides, his attention was concentrated elsewhere.

I reluctantly opened the second, smaller box. The smell reminded me of the torture chamber in which we found the remains of Celia Potter. My hands trembled as I pulled away the cotton wool padding. I almost dropped the box when I saw what lay underneath. 'Oh, God!' I groaned.

We all peered down at the object. It was about the size of a walnut, but generally smooth, although tiny veins and channels were clearly visible. Decent sized tubes were connected at each end, hacked off in clean strikes of the knife. Blood had congealed into a brown sticky mass around it.

'What is that?' asked John.

Well, I had an idea, but I wasn't certain. Biology was never my strongest subject. I looked at Jordan. I think we both recognised it. I replaced the cotton wool and closed the box. Making sure there were no further 'presents' in my locker, I collected my clothes and shoved them into a bag. Slamming the locker door I said, 'We'd better go see Garratt, tell him the good news.'

'You handled these!' he shouted, horrified, glaring at the two boxes sitting on his table. 'I don't believe it!' We remained silent, trying not to think about the lectures we'd endured on the importance of not contaminating a crime scene. We already had enough fingerprints to condemn Arnold, but additional confirmation that he'd broken into the station might have proved useful.

I nodded defiantly. Well, I intended to nod defiantly. Actually, it was more of a solitary embarrassed dip of the head.

After a deep sigh, Garratt asked, 'And you found them in your locker?'

'Yes.'

'How the hell did he get in?'

Silence.

'Allison?'

I held out my hands and shook my head. 'I...'

'Where do you keep your locker key?' he demanded.

'In my belt when I'm on duty.'

He looked at me doubtfully. 'So?'

'Well...'

'Yes?'

'Sometimes when I know I'm going to be in the station all day, I just keep my bag with me.'

'Like when you're in the collator's office?' he asked.

He had a point. 'Yeah.'

'That's why we have rules,' he pointed out, shaking his head.

After a few moments silence, John asked, 'So are you trying to tell me that Arnold was planning all this months ago?'

'I don't think he's the type to miss an opportunity, especially if Allison and Cathy offended him.'

I sighed.

'So, does this mean he's got your house keys as well?' John demanded.

'Yes... I mean no,' I corrected myself quickly. 'It was before I moved to the flat and all the locks have been changed anyway.'

'Well that's something.' Garratt sighed. 'What's in these boxes, then?' he demanded, pointing at them. There was no immediate response. 'Well, take the lids off for God's sake. I don't want *my* fingerprints on them as well.'

I removed the lid of the shoebox and revealed the bulk of Jordan's hair. Garratt looked at her and shook his head. She looked sullen and dejected. Then I lifted the lid of the smaller box and peeled away the cotton wool. Garratt's shoulders dropped. With his head tilted to one side, he pointed and asked, 'What is that?' When no-one answered, he picked up the phone and rang reception. 'Is Professor Stewart still in the building?' he asked.

John smiled in recognition of the man's name. Of all the pathologists police officers came across during the course of their duties, Stewart was the most popular, with the men at any rate. His enormous girth was matched by a sense of humour they found highly amusing but which frequently offended female officers.

'Could you ask him to come to DI Garratt's office immediately.' Putting down the phone, he informed us, 'He'll be up shortly.'

'Are we still going away?' I asked.

'Yes. The sooner the better,' he confirmed.

I started hesitantly. 'I'm not asking you to tell us the address or anything, but please tell me it isn't included on any computer file anywhere.'

'That's what's taking so long,' he informed us. 'Everything has to be done by telephone or face to face: no emails. The Chief Super isn't answering his phone and nobody seems to know where he is. We've made some progress at the destination end.' He took a deep breath. 'Everything should be ready for tomorrow.'

We were interrupted by a knock on the door. Professor Stewart entered the room encased in a smart dark blue suit and MCC tie. His trousers stopped short of his ankles by some distance, like he was wearing them at half-mast. 'You wanted to see me, old man?' he enquired.

'Yes. Have a seat. We'd like you to...'

'John!' cried the professor exceedingly loudly. 'How are you, you old sod?'

John nodded in greeting. 'I'm fine,' he replied smiling.

'How's the testicle?'

I looked sharply at John. He'd stopped smiling and was looking distinctly embarrassed. 'Fine, thank you,' he assured him.

'And the head?'

'Fine.'

I noted that John no longer appeared very talkative.

'You should be careful. Fractured skulls can be very unpleasant, you know, cause any manner of aberrant behaviour. Still, in your case, I suppose it would be difficult to tell, eh?' he chuckled.

John tried to force a smile.

'I thought it was particularly odious what those girls did to his tackle. Huh?' He smirked at me, assuming I knew. He paused, smirking. 'You must be counting your lucky stars, young lady!'

I looked up sharply. He was still addressing me. 'What?'

'Oh, sorry! You not his...? Sorry, didn't know. My apologies. Course, it's not that much of a problem, one's as good as two if you know what I mean.' He looked down at his enormous stomach. 'Course, I haven't been able to see my tackle in years, more's the pity.' There was a long silence as we all reflected on his revelations. 'Anyway,' he went on, addressing me. 'What can I do for you? Does it entail a rigorous physical examination?'

'No!'

'Pity!' He shook his head sadly.

Unwilling to engage in further dialogue, I pushed the small box towards him. As he took it up, Garratt groaned: another set of fingerprints. 'Can you tell me what this is?' I asked.

Not taking his eyes from me, he pulled off the lid. Only after some moments did he look down at the contents. Removing the cotton wool, he took a deep breath, his demeanour immediately becoming serious. 'Ah!' He then picked up the object irreverently by a protruding tube and dangled it in front of his face like a pendulum. 'You're not very familiar with your own body are you young lady?'

'It's not mine!' I hastily assured him.

He let fly a chuckle. 'It's an ovary.'

'Human?'

'Very probably. Might I ask how you came by it?'

'It was left in my locker.'

'Rather superfluous, I would have thought.' He pondered for a moment. 'Why would anyone think you needed it?'

'It's a threat.'

'You should go to the police,' he joked.

I gave him an impatient stare. 'Is there anything else you can tell me?'

'Well, you see this little dangly bit?' I nodded. 'Someone's body used to be connected to that.'

I sighed. 'Is it like... you know... testicles. What you said earlier.' I wasn't enjoying the subject of the discussion. 'What I mean is... Is one enough?'

'Oh yes, I'd have thought so, wouldn't you? Inbuilt redundancy, and all that. Same reason you have two kidneys, two eyes and two hearts. Yes, any woman could get by with only one ovary. It's just as well, really.'

'Why?'

'Well, it means the owner of this one could still be alive.' He looked around the table at the glum faces. 'I guess not! An ovary is not essential for, what's the word they use on *Star Trek*? Life support! That's it.'

I didn't smile. 'Two hearts?'

'Just checking to see whether you were paying attention.'

Professor Stewart departed with the ovary as soon as the chain of evidence details had been established. 'There's something else, isn't there?' Garratt asked, observing our discomfort.

Jordan and I looked at each other and said nothing. John

remained silent. It wasn't his business.

'I can assure you there's no reason to be shy.' He withdrew a clear evidence bag from his top drawer and passed it across the table. It contained an envelope and in front of it, a Polaroid showing Jordan and me linked together on the bed in what could have been a lover's embrace. It could have been ecstasy that held our eyes so tightly shut, but all those around the table knew better. 'I found it in my pigeon hole this morning.'

I closed my eyes, for some reason feeling deeply ashamed. Jordan apparently had no such reservations and appeared a great deal more content than she had since the discovery of her hair. She passed on her photo, which Garratt glanced at before inserting it in a bag. He kept hold of the bag, not closing it, looking expectantly at me. Reluctantly, I slid my hand into my pocket and pushed the picture across the table, face down. Garratt placed it in the envelope without comment, but not before taking a brief glance.

'Is that everything?' he asked.

We nodded.

'Right...'

We were interrupted by a knock at the door. A smart detective, who I knew by sight, entered. 'I've got some of the info you wanted,' he told Garratt, leaving him the option of asking us to leave.

After a brief pause, Garratt replied, 'Go ahead.'

'We've traced Arnold's father. He lives in Surbiton. That's his address.' He handed over a small slip of paper. 'We've also traced two of his fellow students at the seminary. One of them's in Rome, but he's awaiting your call. The other's at a church in Croydon.' He passed over another two slips.

'Telephone records?' Garratt asked.

'We've got them. We're checking them now.'

'Okay, thanks.' He departed and Garratt looked over at us, idly fingering the slips of paper, deciding what to do next. We were making progress. Then I noticed that he was staring at John who, I then discovered, was fast asleep in his chair. 'Let's use the conference room,' he suggested.

Two doors down, we reconvened, leaving John in peace. I think we'd all forgotten the injuries he'd sustained. They were evidently taking their toll. He should have been home in bed recuperating.

'Right!' exclaimed Garratt. 'Let's get started. Grab a handset.' Jordan and I were listening as he dialled the lengthy number in Rome.

'Ciao?' came a muffled response.

'I'd like to speak to Father Williams, please,' replied Garratt.

I thought he was being a little optimistic, and I smiled to myself when he was subjected to a lengthy response in Italian, delivered with startling rapidity.

'Sacerdote Williams, per favore,' Jordan reeled off smoothly. Another of her talents about which I'd been unaware.

There was a long pause, before Father Williams announced his presence. 'Yes, hello,' he shouted.

'Father Williams?' Garratt asked.

'Yes, what can I do for you?'

'Detective Inspector Garratt. I'd like to ask you some questions about someone who attended seminary with you, Lawrence Arnold.'

'Good Lord!' he exclaimed. 'That was a lifetime ago!'

'I appreciate that it's nearly thirty years, but do you remember him?'

'Of course I do! He was a real oddball.'

'How so?'

He took a moment to think. 'He was a real loner. I think he had some sort of communication problem. Never looked you in the eye when he spoke to you. And he was totally incapable of empathy!' He fell silent for a moment, before summing up. 'I can't imagine anyone less suited to the priesthood.'

'Why was he so unsuitable?' Garratt probed.

'Don't get me wrong, he was exceptionally knowledgeable. He could recite the scriptures and Catholic dogma like an encyclopaedia... Oh, yes! He had this way of reciting the martyred saints' details: like an automaton, name, place of death and method. It was quite extraordinary.'

'Saints?' Garratt continued.

'Yes. I never understood why they were so important to him, but he knew them all.' He paused again. 'Ultimately though, it was his lack of compassion that made him so unsuitable.'

'How did that manifest itself?'

'Well, I'll give you an example: we used to have sessions of debate, when you had to take up positions for and against some of the more contentious Catholic dogma. He was completely incapable of formulating an opinion opposed to the Church. For him, dogma was as far as it went. Everything else must be wrong. He just wasn't able to put himself into the shoes of an opposing point of view.'

'Interesting!'

'Can you imagine him in the confessional? What would

he do if one of his parishioners confessed to using contraception? He was totally incapable of a sympathetic response.' He paused a moment.

'So he wouldn't have made the priesthood?'

'No,' he sounded adamant. 'We would have found something for him within the church, but the priesthood, never!'

'Were you surprised about his relationship with the girl?'

Again, he paused to think. 'Not entirely. I always got the impression... I might be wrong...'

'Yes?'

'I always thought that it wasn't him who chose the priesthood. I thought that someone else was behind it and he just went along with it. He must have known he wasn't suited.' After a contemplatory pause, he added, 'Nowadays, they'd probably tell you he had some sort of syndrome. Back then we just thought he was odd.'

'Do you remember the girl's name?'

'Oh...'

'It would help,' Garratt urged.

'I never actually met her,' he replied. 'Sue, Suzy, something like that, I think.'

'Do you remember exactly when this was?'

'Let me think... 1965 we started there, in September. Lawrence didn't stay long... That's right! It was just after the New Year. He must have left in January 1966. I was told his family disowned him. I have no idea what became of him after that.'

'You've been a great help,' Garratt told him. 'One last question: did he have any friends at the seminary? Anyone he was close to?'

'I think he was always suspicious... No, wait! He had one

friend: Jeremy Woolcraft, used to hang around with him a lot of the time. Of course, Woolcraft made it to the priesthood. Very successful he's been.'

'And you've had no further contact with Arnold since?'

'Good heavens, no!'

Garratt thanked him for his time and finished the conversation. We were silent for a good ten minutes as he scribbled his notes, trying not to forget anything. Jordan and I both read his finished transcript and added a couple of items he'd forgotten. Then he summoned a secretary to have them typed and added to the file.

'Woolcraft?' I asked.

'As luck would have it, he's our other priest, in Croydon,' Garratt told me.

'We need to pay him a visit,' Jordan suggested.

'We have an appointment at ten tomorrow.' He looked at his watch. People outside were beginning to pack up and go home. I hadn't realised it was so late.

'We'd better get going,' he told us.

'Where?' I asked.

'We're going to pay Arnold's father a surprise visit.'

Garratt departed to make arrangements. 'Where's your vest?' Jordan suddenly demanded

I looked up, preoccupied, still trying to absorb what Father Williams had told us. 'You sound like my mother.' When I looked up moments later, Jordan was still staring at me. 'I haven't worn a vest since I went to primary school,' I told her.

Jordan's patience was wearing thin. 'Bulletproof vest!' she told me pointedly.

'Oh! I don't have one.'

'You must have a stab vest.'

'Yeah. It's in my locker.'

Jordan sighed in annoyance. 'What good is it there?'

'You haven't got one on,' I pointed out.

'No-one's trying to kill me!'

'Well, it's in my locker protecting my uniform against knife-wielding maniacs.'

'And your picture of John,' Jordan remarked sourly.

I turned to her surprised. 'I don't have a picture of John.'

'On your locker door.'

I frowned. 'Well, I didn't put it there.'

Jordan remained sceptical.

Garratt returned dangling a set of car keys. 'Let's go!'

'What about John?' I asked.

We all craned our heads to see into his office: John was still fast asleep, now slumped on the desk. We decided to go without him. On the way out, we passed the officer who was checking Arnold's phone records and stopped to look at the brightly highlighted pages. 'Anything?' Garratt asked.

He looked up, still grasping a pink highlighter. 'These are to his father. There's a lot.'

'Every week?'

'Sometimes twice or three times. These others, green, are to St Peters rectory: same address I gave you for the priest.'

'Woolcraft?'

'That's right.'

'Interesting!'

It was clear that more work needed to be done and before we departed, Garratt requested phone records from Arnold's father and Father Woolcraft.

Chapter 12

We completed the short drive to Surbiton in little over an hour. With Jordan navigating, we quickly located Arnold's father's house and pulled up outside. It was a very respectable pre-war, semi-detached family home with a small front garden. The grass was ankle high and liberally spotted with weeds, including some towering thistles. The house itself looked in good shape, although a certain amount of litter had escaped from the nearby bins. Garratt took the lead and knocked heavily on the front door.

'What do you want?' an unshaven man with wild grey hair demanded.

'Are you Anthony Arnold?' Garratt asked over-politely.

'Who wants to know?' the man's nose was growing redder by the second, and we hadn't even introduced ourselves yet.

'I'm Detective Inspector Garratt. This is Sergeant Lassiter and WPC Cousins. Can we come in?'

'What for?'

'We need to talk to you.'

'What about?'

'Your son, Lawrence.'

'That useless piece of crap! What's he done now?'

'Is he here?' Garratt demanded.

'I haven't seen him for months,' he was told.

'Can we come in?' Garratt repeated.

Reluctantly, he led us into a hallway that looked like it hadn't seen a duster for decades. He ushered us into the front room, but not before we caught a glimpse of the kitchen, which looked like the scene of a small explosion. An unpleasant odour of decaying vegetation emanated from the room. I fancied I caught sight of fleeting motion around the skirting board. He indicated a sofa that was held together largely by the layers of grease clogging its threadbare fabric. Discarded newspapers littered the floor and a central table was stacked with empty bottles and cans. His tipple of choice appeared to be continental lager with a cheap blended whiskey chaser.

Garratt took a look around and suggested, 'Perhaps we'd be more comfortable at the station.'

'Are you arresting me?' he asked in horror.

'Don't tempt me!'

'What for?'

'Crimes against housekeeping.'

Arnold sighed and led us across the hall into what appeared to be an unused dining room. 'Haven't been in here for years,' he told us. He sat down and placed his arms on the table, leaving a dark streak where the dust had been disturbed.

'We need to speak to you about your son, Lawrence,' Garratt repeated.

'My son... What can I tell you about my son?' He considered the prospect for some time before continuing. 'When everyone's kissing his arse, there's not a problem in the world. When people make fun of him, it's best to run for the hills.' He threw his hands in the air, imitating some sort of blast. 'Not immediately you understand, he'll take his time, but when he gets his revenge, it's like a visit from hell. Nobody's safe. All those years in America, he was top dog. Nobody else could do what he did. He was untouchable.'

That was news to us, but we needed to take matters in a logical order. 'Before you go on,' Garratt interceded. 'Perhaps you could start from the seminary. He was only there about five months.'

'That's about right! Old days every family's useless son became a priest. He couldn't even get that right!'

'There was a girl involved,' Garratt suggested.

'Yeah! Threw away his career for a bit of skirt.'

'Do you remember the girl's name?' I asked.

'That little trollop!' he cast his mind back. 'Suzy or something similar. Nearly ruined him! Reported him to the police!'

'Second name?'

He thought for a moment. 'Never knew it,' he replied unconvincingly.

Garratt took over once again. 'Could you take us through the chronology.'

'Chronology?'

'We know he left the seminary early in 1966. What did he do after that?'

'I kicked his arse out!'

Garratt sighed. 'I understand that, but what did Lawrence do?'

'Didn't have any money. He crashed out at one of his friends. Slept on the sofa!'

'Then what?'

'He got a temp job. That was when the first computers were coming out. His company bought one to control its machinery. Kept going wrong!' he exclaimed. 'Guess who was the only one who could fix it? Didn't matter what it was – Lawrence had the gift.'

'So I understand,' Garratt said.

'He enrolled at the local college, but the teachers were worse than useless. After a few months, Lawrence was teaching them!' Despite his tendency to denigrate his son, it was clear that he was a proud father. 'Never finished his course! He was head-hunted by some computer company and never looked back.'

'So...' Garratt attempted to stem the flow.

'Then he had to go and get married. Hardly knew the girl! Didn't know what love is, he didn't!' He sat back in his chair and grinned. 'Just couldn't see it, could he?' He lapsed into silence.

'Couldn't see what?' I felt compelled to ask.

He threw out his hands. 'He's not the marrying kind! Only ever thinks of himself. She wanted kids. Desperate she was. He found out soon enough that he preferred being on his own. He got himself sent all over the country: long contracts. He was away for months at a time.' He leaned forward and whispered confidentially, 'She wasn't the kind to be happy alone, if you know what I mean!'

'So you're suggesting that she was unfaithful?' Garratt asked.

'I think you could say that. Not immediately, you understand, but after a couple of years, she gave up on Lawrence.'

'How did the marriage end?' I asked.

He sighed. 'She died in a house fire. Lawrence was away on a job at the time.'

Garratt scribbled in his notebook. 'What did he do then?'

'Went to America, he did,' he told us.

'How long did he stay?'

'Oh... Years. Seven, eight, I have no idea really.'

'He did well there?'

'They loved him there. He was the king! Gave him posh houses with big swimming pools to live in. Employed staff to cook and clean up after him. They couldn't do enough for him.' He took a moment to think. 'You know all these big computer companies now? Who do you think it was that built the foundations? Huh?' We didn't respond, despite seeing where he was going. 'Lawrence, that's who!'

'So why did he leave?'

'Got a better offer! All of a sudden, the games industry was where it's at. And who took the lead in that? The Japs. They needed him there. So he went. Nearly three years he spent there.'

'And then what?'

He shook his head sadly. 'Came back home after that. I think...'

'Why?'

'He was never the same after that,' he informed us miserably. 'I don't know what happened. Japs probably pushed him too hard... When he came back, he just lay around all day. I figure he had some sort of mental breakdown.'

'Where did he stay in England?' Garratt asked.

'With me, of course.'

'You forgave him, then?'

'Yeah, well. Blood's thicker and all that.'

'And he'd made lots of money,' I pointed out.

'Didn't know what to do with it all. He bought me this house.'

'He did?'

'Yeah! He had stacks of money just sitting around. He had no idea! I told him property was always a good buy.'

'And he's been here ever since?' Garratt continued.

'No!' Anthony cried. 'After about six months, he buggered off again. I didn't think it was a good idea.'

'Why not?'

'He wasn't well! Something inside him broke when he was in Japan!'

'But he went anyway?'

'Yes, Canada this time, but not in the tech industry. Some drug company. He worked in-house. The pace was much slower.'

'So he never returned to the industry?'

'Look! Nothing lasts forever. He was good, maybe brilliant, but it's a young man's game. He was over forty and still the young kids were coming to him for advice. Then they all stopped coming. Fell off his perch. Came back home with his tail between his legs.' He thought for a moment. 'He's still good though; just not special anymore. No problem getting a job. He's still in demand.'

Garratt wanted to plant the suggestion that Lawrence was dangerous. 'We think he's now active in England, killing people,' he told him.

He considered Garratt's suggestion for a few moments. It didn't seem to surprise him. 'Then, my advice to you is "Don't piss him off!"' he finally responded with a bronchial laugh.

We all had a lot to think about during the drive back. Jordan was uncharacteristically quiet. Despite repeatedly pressing him, we all came away from the interview knowing full well that Anthony hadn't been very forthcoming. He'd been very careful about what he told us. He clearly hadn't revealed the whole truth and we would have to conduct further interviews with him.

Jordan and I sat outside Garratt's office. 'Where's John?' I asked no-one in particular. I felt a pang of guilt at not having thought about him for so long. Jordan shrugged in a familiar manner, indicating her lack of interest in the subject. I picked up the phone and called Paul Bodin's mobile number. He'd probably left for the day, but I thought he might be able to help.

'Hi, Allison,' he responded after I identified myself.

'Where are you?' I asked.

'Err, home!' he replied sarcastically. 'It's half past eight.'

'Can you do something for me?'

After a brief hesitation, he replied, 'Of course, if I can.'

'I'm looking for a dead girl,' I told him. 'Name's Sue or Susan or Suzy, anything like that.'

'When?' he asked.

'Any time in the last twenty-eight years,' I told him.

There was a long delay. 'Right...'

'But,' I continued. 'I think you can narrow the area to Cumbria, somewhere near the seminary.'

'Where was that?'

It wasn't an unreasonable question, but I didn't have the answer. 'Don't know! Give me the whole of Cumbria.'

'You know that twenty-eight years ago, we didn't have computers,' he told me in a patronising tone.

'I know, Paul, but you're very resourceful.'

'How do you know?'

I had to think quickly. 'Garratt told me.'

'Hmm.' He didn't sound convinced. 'I'll get back to you. Where will you be?'

'Right here at the station, custody suite,'

He paused a beat. 'Have you been arrested?'

'Not yet! It's for my own protection.'

'Right!'

He rang off. When I glanced around, Jordan had disappeared. I'm sure she wasn't too far away, but she wasn't in my line of sight. Garratt was busy on another phone, so I sat there thinking about Anthony Arnold. It sounded like Lawrence's father had given him a hard time growing up.

I thought of Trevor and his current predicament. My parents were still happily married and would soon be celebrating their thirtieth anniversary, but my father hadn't managed to pass on the secrets of being a good husband to his son. I could remember when we were young and Dad used to put us to bed. Trevor would look up at him with awestruck eyes and tell him, 'Daddy, you know everything. What will I do when you die?' Dad would then patiently explain that it was his job to pass on that knowledge, and that Trevor would know everything he needed to know by the time he got old. As luck would have it, Dad's still alive and kicking. I guess in the case of Trevor at least, the education is still ongoing.

I called my mother, remembering that I still hadn't talked to Trevor about Sharon. I'd been a little preoccupied! She answered and we had a short conversation. She was getting used to being left at home while the men went out in the evening.

Jordan returned and sat opposite me. 'John's in hospital,' she told me.

I looked up sharply. 'What?'

She shook her head. 'It's nothing, delayed concussion or something. They're keeping him in overnight to be sure. He'll be out tomorrow.'

'I should go and see him.'

'Leave him alone! He's in the best place.'

I thought she was probably right, but I would still have liked to see him. I was sure there was something we should be doing in our search for Lawrence Arnold. I just wasn't sure what it was. Officers continued to examine various telephone records and if they found something incriminating, Garratt would be the first to know. It's strange to reflect that during that time, I wasn't the least concerned for my own safety. We'd gone out to meet Arnold's father without a second thought, never suspecting that there could be a murderer sheltering in the house. I suppose subconsciously I thought that he'd never get a better chance to kill me than the previous night, and he hadn't.

Eventually, Garratt finished scribbling a record of the interview and offered the sheets to us. Jordan went first and made a whole host of pencilled additions. It was difficult to believe that anything could have been overlooked by the time it made its way into my hands. I gave it a cursory read before handing it back. Garratt put it in a tray for a typist, then announced his intention to go home. He escorted us to the custody suite, delivered various instructions, then left us.

It would be wrong to dwell on that night. Garratt had done what he thought was best and we both survived to tell the tale. I *did* feel compelled to point out to him that there was no hot water, the mattresses weren't comfortable and by the time our food was delivered from the canteen, it certainly wasn't hot. We did however receive some fresh clothing from our respective flats, so at least we could change.

When I awoke, Jordan was standing over me protectively. She seemed lost in thought. The barred window was aglow with sunshine and I was surprised to notice that it was after nine. After groaning a little, I suggested, 'We'd better get going. We have a ten o'clock appointment.'

She nodded.

We staggered up to Garratt's office where he was busy on the phone. Finally he slammed it down angrily. 'We've been bumped,' he told us.

'Why?'

'Father Woolcraft is ministering to the family of two of his parishioners who were killed in a car accident last night. We're seeing him at two.'

Jordan and I both sat, deflated. Surely another morning wasn't going to pass with no progress? 'Are we still going away?' I asked.

'Yes!' he said hurriedly. 'I'm nearly there. We have a location and I'm just awaiting final authorisation to proceed.'

I nodded. Jordan scratched her ear. 'Why can't we stay here a few days?' she asked.

He took a moment to collect his thoughts. 'I can't do it,' he told us finally. 'The DCI wouldn't approve it.' So, clearly he'd thought the same. 'He told me this was a police station, not a hotel.' He sighed wearily. 'We've got three coming in tonight for their court hearings in the morning and the weekend's coming up.' He held his hands out in futility. 'Besides, you'll be safer away from here. Arnold seems to come and go as he pleases. It's too dangerous.'

He evidently saw something in Jordan's expression that demanded explanation. 'What are you thinking, Jordan?'

She seemed reluctant to explain, but eventually admitted, 'I was thinking about Professor Stern.'

'Jordan!' he warned.

She just shrugged.

'It's not a good idea.'

'Who's Professor Stern?' I asked when it became apparent that no-one was going to elaborate.

'Psychologist,' Jordan told me.

'You're talking about a profiler?'

Jordan tilted her head to one side. 'He has a reputation. He might be able to help.'

'Reputation for what?' Garratt mumbled.

'It's not like we have anything else to do,' she pointed out.

'I'll have to assign protection!' he exclaimed.

'Couple of officers.'

He sighed a long sigh, but eventually he agreed. I think he felt that getting us out from under his feet would allow him to do some work. He didn't want us hanging around aimlessly. He teamed us up with a pair of officers and we departed for Queen Mary College in East London.

Having managed successfully to leave the two uniforms at the entrance, we approached the reception desk. Immediately a bright young lady sprung forward. Her badge indicated that her name was Judy. She had trouble taking her eyes off Jordan's shaved head. She swept her own flowing blonde locks out of her eyes and asked, 'Can I help you?'

'We're looking for Professor Stern,' Jordan told her.

She blew out her cheeks. 'He's just started a lecture I'm afraid.'

'Oh hell!' Jordan exclaimed.

'I know,' she remarked sympathetically. 'You could speak to him after.'

'Right,' Jordan replied with resignation. 'Come on.' She grabbed my arm and pulled me towards the lecture theatre. We entered a steeply banked auditorium with space for about two hundred people. I counted eleven. We sat towards the back and tried to ignore the sighing and pained expressions of our fellow attendees.

Nearly an hour later, Jordan prodded me in the ribs. I was surprised to discover that I was sound asleep. Judging by the dazed motions of the rest of the students, so were they. We descended and approached a thin, balding man, whose remaining grey hair sprouted generously around the ears, and nowhere else. His wire rimmed glasses perched precariously on the tip of his nose. He gave us a welcoming smile and asked what he could do for us. Jordan introduced us and then he turned to me.

'Did you enjoy my lecture?' he asked with a smile. His accent was strong: Eastern Europe I thought.

I looked round, not sure what to say. I was conscious of his eyes burning into me. 'Yeah,' I replied confidently. 'It was... I was particularly interested in...' I realised I had no idea what it was about, '...bits of it.'

'Really? Which bits?' he persisted.

I looked at Jordan for help, but she was shamelessly reading a note on the professor's desk. 'Well, the... interesting bits.' I looked up at him and returned his smile.

He looked at me suspiciously then turned his attention to Jordan who stopped reading and looked up. 'And what about you, young lady?'

'Yeah,' she replied uninterested. 'Been there.'

'You've attended one of my lectures before?'

'Yeah.'

'I hope it helped.'

'Yeah, cured my insomnia.'

'You're very rude,' he said.

'I'd rather be rude than boring,' she replied icily.

'Jordan!' I appealed.

'What?'

'Stop being rude!'

She shrugged. 'It's what I do best, remember?'

I turned angrily towards her. 'I'm sure the other students found it very interesting.'

'Name me three,' she replied instantly.

'What?'

'Name me three students who found it interesting.'

'How am I supposed to name them! I don't know any of them.'

'There you are then,' she responded.

'Christ! You can be such a cow!'

The three of us looked at each other in turn. Jordan appeared rather hurt. The professor turned to her. 'And this is one of your *friends*?' he said in alarm.

'I *used* to think so.'

I suddenly got the impression that there was more going on here than I understood. 'Wait a minute. You two are taking the piss, right?'

'What is this?' the professor asked Jordan. 'Taking the piss?'

'It's a crude, vulgar expression not normally heard in polite conversation.'

'Yeah, well, you'd know all about that,' I replied spitefully.

'You have guts, young lady. Maybe you are just what Jordan needs.'

'For what?' I asked.

He looked at me with a smirk. 'For a friend.'

I wasn't convinced. 'How do you two know each other?'

'Jordan once arrested my wife.'

'What for?' I asked surprised.

'Murder.'

'Whose murder?'

'Mine,' he replied.

I looked at Jordan who had the good grace to look embarrassed. 'He wasn't dead,' she pointed out quietly.

'I can see that.'

'He should have been,' she mused.

'But God was not prepared to let me go!' he said triumphantly. 'He said I have more boring lectures to deliver, more children to anaesthetise with my words. So he let me live.'

'You don't seem to have a very high opinion of yourself,' I suggested.

'I have an immensely high opinion of myself! I don't think it would be unfair for anyone to call me a genius. But I am *very* boring! And you know why? Because nobody understands my ideas. Not even me! Anybody who stays awake during my lectures isn't listening properly!'

'So, it was attempted murder, your wife?'

'Yes!'

'That must have been very difficult. Your wife...'

'No, not really!' he interrupted. 'It wasn't my wife!'

I looked at Jordan, who was busy studying the overhead projector. 'You got the wrong person too?' I asked.

Jordan shrugged. 'I was new.'

He shook his head in sympathy. He evidently didn't hold

any grudges. 'So, what can I do for you?'

'We have a situation,' she told him.

'You'd better come to my office.'

Jordan explained the situation in excruciating detail, highlighting any and all of our suspicions against Arnold. Many were mere speculation, but overall she presented a very detailed modus operandi. Stern responded throughout with questions and reactions that proved that he was absorbing every detail.

'Hmm,' he responded when Jordan finished. 'It is not normal.'

'Damn right, it's not normal!' I told him.

'No, young lady, I'm not referring to his actions, I'm referring to the chronology. Something is missing.'

'Twenty-eight years?' I suggested.

'Yes, of course. I think... this is not new for him. It's a technique he has already perfected. Somewhere there are more bodies, his early work. Now he will go on killing until he's had enough.'

'You make it sound like he'll want to be caught.'

'At some point, yes. He'll want recognition. Your perpetrator, Arnold, is not yet at that point, I think, but he will want his work to be recognised.'

'We're checking with the American and Japanese authorities for any unsolved murders following the same MO,' Jordan told him.

'Yes! Either there are bodies hidden somewhere or...'

'Yes,' I prompted.

'Sometimes... they think they're working for a higher power.' He fell silent.

'Yes?' I grew tired waiting.

'It could explain…'

'What?' I demanded loudly. Jordan tutted and shook her head. 'What?' I repeated, this time to her.

'Let him think,' she told me quietly.

We sat for several minutes in icy silence while the professor ran through the permutations in his brain. Jordan pulled faces either to poke fun at the professor or just to lighten the mood. It didn't work.

'Yes, I think so,' he finally concluded.

I remained silent and crossed my arms. This time it was Jordan who prompted him. 'Would you care to share your conclusions?' she asked unusually politely.

'The chronology is all wrong,' he stated simply. 'He is not working alone. There's someone else: someone he respects.'

'His father?' I suggested.

'Could be,' he replied unconvinced.

'How does it work?' Jordan asked.

'Many killers, they say they hear voices in their heads,' he told us waving his hands around frantically. 'Some, of course, are mentally ill, but some truly believe they are following instructions. They can't, or won't, identify the voices, but they believe they are following orders. I think…' He fell silent again.

'What!?' I demanded, louder than I intended.

He shook his head sadly in my direction. 'Such impatience!' he remarked to Jordan. She nodded her head in agreement. 'You say he's a religious man?'

'Yes, he was in a seminary.'

'Was there someone?' He looked at us expectantly. 'A fellow priest, perhaps? Someone he looked up to?'

That was a good question and we would find the answer to it that very afternoon.

Chapter 13

When we arrived back at Garratt's office, John was waiting. He'd been discharged, but told him to take it easy. He opted out of the trip to Father Woolcraft, and went to collect some clothes for our imminent journey into hiding. No-one had yet confirmed he was coming, so I thought he was being a little over-optimistic. Jordan also chose not to come with us. In her case, the reason was more practical: she was collecting a firearm.

I wasn't great company on the journey, falling asleep as soon as we hit the major roads. Garratt shook my shoulder as we came to a stop beneath a very modern church spire. 'This it?' I asked.

'St Peter's,' he replied. 'Let's find Father Woolcraft.'

I dragged myself out of the car and followed in his wake. It was early afternoon and it was unlikely there were any services to conduct. Hopefully, he'd finished consoling the bereaved and he'd have some time to talk. I lingered in the porch gazing at the literature pinned to a large corkboard as Garratt strode ahead. The flyers had details of mass times and church social events; nothing remotely interesting. I spotted a small picture. It was about the size and shape of a playing card and depicted a stern, unattractive woman swathed in a scarlet shawl and headscarf. An obligatory halo hovered over her head, and she stood in front of what looked like a golden screen. She was holding some sort of bottle or jar in her right hand. Her left hand was offered up in blessing. I wasn't sure what to make of it, so after making sure no-one was watching, I slipped it into my pocket.

When I entered the church, Garratt was already chatting to a good-looking grey haired gentleman with a dog collar. 'Father Woolcraft, this is Allison Cousins,' Garratt said.

'Pleased to meet you, young lady.' I nodded my greeting and took a moment to study his ready smile. He was charming: if he was my priest, I might go to church more often. 'Let's go somewhere more comfortable, shall we?'

We followed him through a plain wooden door into a room lit by lamps held in ornamental sconces. He took his place at the head of the table. 'So, Lawrence Arnold,' he started.

'Yes,' replied Garratt. 'We're interested in anything you can tell us.'

He shook his head ruefully. 'It was a long time ago, but I'll do my best.'

'Before we start,' Garratt continued. 'Is there any sort of confidentiality problem?'

'No,' he replied simply. We looked at each other, confused. After all, this was the Catholic Church. 'When I last saw Lawrence, he told me that someone would come and that I was to tell them everything. He said I was his witness and the truth had to come out.'

'Wait!' demanded Garratt. 'When did you last see Arnold?'

'Oh, a couple of months ago now.' He waved his hand dismissively. 'He was just passing and dropped in to say hello.'

'Just passing!' Garratt scoffed.

Woolcraft looked confused. 'Is he in some sort of trouble?'

'You could say that.' Garratt scratched his head. 'We need

to know exactly what happened all those years ago.'

'Right. Well, I've been trying to remember all the details.'

'You were friends?' Garratt suggested.

'Oh, yes. We were both in the same boat, of course: arrived fresh in the seminary on the same day. We both had such high hopes.'

'You seem to have been a success,' Garratt remarked.

'Not really. I'm still a priest.' He shook his head. 'If I could have chosen anyone I met at the seminary to become a successful priest, it would have been Lawrence. He was perfect for the role: incredibly knowledgeable and totally committed. He would have made a fine priest.'

Garratt and I just looked at him doubtfully. 'Would it surprise you to know that we've been told the exact opposite by someone else who attended with Arnold?'

'What? Who?'

'We were told,' Garratt went on, 'that Arnold was incapable of empathy and unable to construct a simple argument contrary to the Church's beliefs.'

'Well, I don't think...' he started defensively.

'And that he would have been unable to give guidance to his parishioners on controvertial matters and that he was totally unsuited to the priesthood.'

There was a moment's silence. 'Well, it's true that...' He was clearly floundering.

I decided to step in diplomatically. 'Anyway, it all went wrong for him,' I suggested.

He composed himself before giving me a sad smile. 'He wasn't the first priest to be led astray by a young lady.'

'How, if he was so committed?'

'I still find it hard to believe that attractive young ladies were allowed to work in the seminary,' he remarked. 'Even the medical wing.'

'Temptation is an important concept in the New Testament,' I reminded him.

He rewarded me with another smile. 'You're quite right of course, young lady.'

'So, what happened?'

He took a deep breath. 'Lawrence broke his wrist playing cricket. Not a big deal, clean break, just a plaster for a couple of months. But he had to keep checking with the doctor. That's when he met her.'

'A cleaner?'

'Yes, a bright, perky little thing. She fell for him straight away and I can't pretend that he didn't, at least in part, reciprocate her affections. I warned him,' he mused before falling silent. 'It was too dangerous, you see. An innocent friendship can so easily be misinterpreted. By the time he realised she was threatening his vocation, it was already too late.'

'What happened?'

'They… went places together: swimming, the cinema. You get the idea. Suddenly his head was impossibly confused. He was enjoying their friendship which, I believe, was entirely platonic, but it was being noticed and questions were being asked. Finally, he told her that he couldn't see her again. His vocation was more important than her friendship. Besides, she obviously wanted more and Lawrence wasn't exactly marriage material.' Garratt and I shared a glance. 'She took it badly, threatened to tell the Dean that he'd raped her. Lawrence pleaded with her. He even asked me to talk to her at one point.'

'Did you?'

'Yes. I told her how damaging she had become, that she was risking Lawrence's entire future, that there was no way on earth that Lawrence would marry her.'

'How did she respond?'

He looked down. 'I think it was after that she started the campaign,' he muttered.

'What campaign?'

'She did terrible things: silent phone calls, abusive calls, sent him strange, tortured postcards, damaged his clothes, used his cheques. Oh, you name it, she tried it. When all that failed, she reported him to the police for rape.'

'Wait!' exclaimed Garratt. 'This is important. Tell us everything you remember about this campaign against him. We need to know the details.'

He blew out his cheeks. 'It was thirty years ago!' He shook his head. 'I can remember him talking about silent phone calls. He showed me some photos or postcards that he'd received: different types of ancient torture. Some of them were quite horrific. I don't... His cheques were being cashed all over the place. He never had a lot of money, but he spent days at the bank complaining about fraud. Oh! Then his clothes. He actually showed me them. She'd sprayed bleach all over them: completely ruined them. They were unwearable.'

'What did he do then?'

'He went to the Dean and made a clean breast of it, told him everything. The next thing I heard was that the Dean received a very compromising picture of Lawrence.'

'Compromising in what way?'

'Allegedly, he was naked.' Again, Garratt and I exchanged glances. 'Lawrence told me that she'd taken it when he was changing after swimming, but for the Dean, it was the last straw. Lawrence was asked to leave the seminary. It destroyed him.'

There was silence as we reflected on the unsavoury story. Then I was struck by a thought. 'What became of the girl?' I asked.

'Susanna?' he replied. 'I don't know.'

An icy chill gripped my spine. Slowly I delved into my pocket and retrieved the small photo. I pushed it across the table towards Garratt. He took one look and groaned. Saint Susanna glared back at him sternly.

'May I ask what's going on?' Woolcraft requested.

Garratt took a deep breath, before ignoring the question. 'What happened to Arnold after he left the seminary? Do you know?'

'Bits and pieces,' he replied. 'He was completely disowned by his parents. I gather his father was a bit of a Tartar, didn't want to know him.' He shook his head sadly. 'Poor Lawrence had nowhere to go, had to start from scratch. Of course, it didn't take him long to discover that he was some sort of genius.'

Garratt and I exchanged a glance. 'Genius?' I prompted.

'Yes, this was at the birth of the binary age. Within a few years, we had pocket calculators on general sale and games consoles. Personal computers followed soon afterwards. He was a natural. He enroled on some courses and within weeks he was teaching the teachers. He was involved with all those early British electronic gadgets. For several years we led the market. Of course, that didn't last long.'

'What happened?'

'Silicon Valley and the great American takeover happened. I didn't hear from Lawrence for ten years or more.

Difficult to be anonymous in that industry. If you were good, you were headhunted. He went where the work was. I heard he'd got married, but he was always away with some company or other.'

'And he later went to America?' I asked.

'America, yes, later, after his wife died. His child was adopted and he had no real reason to stay. By then, America had taken over and that's where the work was. I think I'm right in saying he also spent time in Canada and Japan.' He looked like he was scouring his memory. 'Maybe Japan's a figment of my imagination. I'm not sure.'

'Did you know his father?' I asked.

'I met him once when he visited the seminary. You couldn't tell then.'

'Tell what?'

'How much of a malign influence he was on Lawrence. He never did anything without his father's approval. Discovering his skills with IT allowed him to break free. His father never bothered him when he was in America. It was only when he came back to England. He bought him a house, you know.'

'Really?' I prompted.

'Yes, but by re-establishing contact with his father, he allowed him back into his life. I suspect he's never left. I advised him to get another job overseas. His influence didn't seem to stretch that far. I thought it might break the spell. For once, he listened. He took a job in Canada for three years.'

'You don't think they were in contact?'

'I really have no idea.'

'And then he came back to London permanently.'

He raised his eyebrows in acknowledgement. 'Don't underestimate the influence of his father.'

Food for thought.

We raced back to Garratt's office buoyed by the news that our transfer to a secret location had finally been given top-level clearance. John had been given a clean bill of health and would be coming with us. The doctors had advised he rest for two weeks followed by a gradual return to work. They hoped that after four weeks, he would be able to resume full duties. Garratt actually suggested that our trip to a safe house would be just what John needed: complete rest and a total lack of stress. Those were his exact words...

While the final preparations were being made, Garratt handed me the telephone. 'Paul,' he told me.

'Hi, Paul. What have you got?'

'I've just had an email. February 1980, Cumbria police reported an unidentified deceased young female: decapitated. Her head was found about twenty yards from her body.'

'She's not unidentified any longer,' I remarked, before adding, 'She's not bright and perky anymore either.'

We still didn't know her full name, but there had to be records, even from thirty years ago. Paul had a great ability to dig up information. He was a computer whiz, but could still ferret out information that wasn't on any hard drive. It was a talent that we would come to rely on.

Before departing for our unknown destination, Jordan provided me with a bulletproof vest. She also gave me strict instructions that I was never to leave the safety of the house, wherever that may be, without it. The vest was heavy and bulky. It made me look four months pregnant and it made me sweat. However, if wearing it kept Jordan happy, I'd put up with it. I didn't drag her all the way back from Rotterdam only to ignore all her advice. I guess you could say I'd learned my lesson. She was in charge and whatever she wanted, I'd make sure she got.

Meanwhile, back in London, events were spiralling rapidly out of control. I'd only learn what happened later, but after the house on Engadene Street was raided and Celia's body discovered, the usual house-to-house enquiries were carried out. One uniformed constable, PC Peebles, had questioned an unassuming gentleman residing at number 61. He was later described as being softly-spoken, middle-aged, medium height, with grey hair and a puffy complexion.

By sending us away, DI Garratt was mounting an operation on another force's turf. Throughout the endless discussions and red tape, he insisted that no traces of our location were *ever* committed to *any* computer. Offices throughout the two regions were sent scurrying for antiquated manual typewriters to prepare documents. Absolutely nothing was to be recorded on the computer. It was a sensible precaution because Arnold had already gained access to the payroll system, supposedly the most secure system of all. Unfortunately, the chain is only as strong as its weakest link.

At Engadene Street, the forensic team worked through the night. I'm told that some of the objects they discovered would have made my hair fall out in horror. And that was only in the upstairs bedroom. The wooden bed frame showed signs of restraints being regularly employed and some of the 'tools' were still mottled with dried blood. However, Celia's fingerprints were mysteriously absent from the room.

By early morning, they'd successfully identified Arnold's

prints and recovered traces of Celia's last agonising hours from the basement. However, they were growing increasingly perplexed. Another set of fingerprints had been recovered from locations throughout the house, including the torture chamber. They were fairly certain they were from a female, but they didn't correspond to Lucy or Celia. So who was indulging in sadistic sport of a horizontal nature upstairs? It raised the ugly spectre of an accomplice, someone who had either willingly, or maybe not-so-willingly, participated in Arnold's twisted games.

Garratt decided to have a chat with Cathy Pollock, the girl who shared an office with Arnold after our embarrassing social gaffe. She'd since moved on and was working near Green Park, from where she'd copied the post-mortem photos I gave Jordan. Apparently, she wasn't very forthcoming at first, maintaining that she'd tried her best to forget ever meeting him.

As Garratt probed further, Cathy admitted that she *had* met Arnold again. It started innocently enough. It was the end of term at college and Cathy, with several others, had gone to a bar to celebrate. By the time Lawrence Arnold sidled over and plonked himself down in a chair next to her, I think it's safe to assume she'd had a few too many. As luck would have it, he was employed on a short-term contract at the college. I also think it's safe to assume that as far as luck went, Cathy's had just run out.

I liked Cathy. She was my age and we'd gone through training together, watching as our colleagues dropped by the wayside. We were both young and homesick and unlike our male counterparts didn't seek solace at the end of a dozen lagers and a dodgy curry. We'd helped each other along.

There were times when we both felt like chucking it in, but we talked it through, encouraging each other, and we'd stuck it out. She was a real friend. She liked similar things and we'd gone out together countless times.

She remained tight-lipped even after Garratt informed her that Arnold was responsible for the deaths of at least two girls. It was only after he told her that my life was in danger that she eventually co-operated.

At closing time, the story went, Cathy looked up through inebriated eyes and couldn't find any of her friends, including the one who was supposed to be giving her a lift home. No problem! Arnold was there and he offered. Despite her unease, she thought him harmless enough. He took her back to his place for coffee. She couldn't remember whether she'd protested or not, but recalled sitting in his living room drinking the coffee. She woke up the next morning with a splitting headache, with which I could sympathise, naked in bed next to him.

Her version of events didn't include any sexual contact, consensual or otherwise. She insisted she hadn't been touched in any way. It came as something of a surprise therefore, when she received an explicit photograph of herself in the post about a week later. Again, I could sympathise. What I couldn't understand was that as a serving police officer, she hadn't immediately reported it. We were clearly missing something, but she swore blind that she hadn't seen him since that night.

Chapter 14

We drove for over two hours in a westerly direction ending up in the middle of nowhere. Our driver was Michael, not Mick or Mickey. He spoke even less than Jordan. I got the impression that the two of them knew each other. I also got the impression that Jordan didn't like him. They frequently exchanged scowls. Maybe it was some form of primitive mating ritual.

We tried to relax. Periodically, John took my hand, but the sight of Jordan's piercing eyes staring back at us didn't encourage intimacy. We drove through the night along endless, faceless motorways. We would have reached our destination sooner had Michael been willing to exceed the speed limit, even marginally. We progressed at a very sober rate, watching other cars zip past us.

It was well past midnight by the time that we began to wend our way through smaller suburban streets. We passed straight through a village, the name of which escaped me as I drifted in and out of an uneasy sleep. John tried to remain alert and follow the signposts, but struggled to stay awake. We were both jolted from sleep when the car started to vibrate as we passed over uneven ground. We'd left the paved roads behind us and were pulling to a halt outside a small farm cottage. As John and I looked around, we saw nothing. In the far distance, a dim sepia glow indicated the presence of a village, but not a single light shone for miles around.

Before we were even out of the car, I could hear Jordan muttering under her breath. From what I managed to catch it was something to do with 'cowboy operations' and 'total incompetence'. Jordan was a professional. When she was allotted the duties of protecting some dignitary, she spent weeks preparing. She analysed the territory in minute detail, evaluating its weaknesses and planning alternative strategies should something go wrong. She put herself into the shoes of a potential assailant and predicted where he would attack. Then she had her counter-strategies in place. Being dumped at a deserted farmhouse in the middle of God knows where wasn't her idea of a safe location.

Jordan strode to the front door and unlocked it, flicking the light switch in the hall. Pools of light formed on the gravel pathway and illuminated a stunted flowerbed. When every room was lit up like a target for anyone within a ten-mile radius, she emerged. 'Inside,' she instructed us. 'Michael will bring the bags.'

Michael didn't appear very impressed by the idea, but started his chore, muttering under his breath. It was obvious who was in charge of this operation. Within an hour we were asleep, while Michael kept watch. John occupied one bedroom and I was across the corridor in another. It wasn't exactly what I had in mind when I'd suggested John came along, but we were too tired to argue with Jordan when she'd assigned the rooms. Neither of us could work out exactly where Jordan spent the night.

We both slept uneasily, despite our fatigue. Come sunrise, the thin floral curtains did little to prevent the sun streaming into my room. I lay on my back staring at the ceiling and listening to the sounds of nature. The trees were filled with the high-pitched songs of birds. It was cold and my room wasn't heated. My breath was a delicate mist as it escaped my lips.

I jumped as a door opened nearby. Seconds later, floorboards started groaning as someone made their way along the corridor.

'Stay in your room!' came Jordan's unmistakable growl.

'Morning, Jordan!' John replied cheerfully. 'I just wanted to see if Allison's okay.'

'She's fine,' she said impatiently.

'I just want to check.'

Jordan took a deep breath. 'You and Allison are... You're together?' she asked. I wished they were talking a little louder. I could only just make out what they were saying.

'Yes,' he replied. '*Very* together!'

I couldn't hear Jordan's response.

'Are you armed?' John asked after a lengthy silence. When he received no response, he asked, 'Are you all right?'

She made no immediate reply. As he gently opened my door, she told him, 'I *am* armed.'

'Hi,' came a whisper as he closed the door behind him. 'How'd you sleep?'

'Not too well,' I replied as I shifted over and allowed him to join me in the cramped single bed. 'Is Jordan okay?'

He thought about it. 'I think she fancies you.'

I punched him playfully on the shoulder. 'Don't!'

'I'm serious! She looked very disappointed when I told her we were together. I told her to keep her hair on!'

'John!' I punched him again, harder this time. 'Leave her alone.'

'She looked very unhappy about me coming in here. I think she's going to try to keep us apart.'

'She won't,' I assured him.

He put his arm around me and we lay back. 'I wonder what we're supposed to do now we're here?'

'Well, I know what I'd like to do,' I said, turning towards him and kissing him. I crawled over him until I was lying on top, our faces close, our noses almost touching.

There was a sharp knock on the door. 'Breakfast!' cried Jordan. 'Downstairs in five minutes.'

We looked at each other and smiled. 'Told you,' whispered John.

Apparently, Jordan had spent the night sitting on the floor, leaning against the banisters. She sat cross-legged like an infant at assembly in primary school. Her position was exactly midway between the two rooms, her line of vision straight down the short corridor. Behind her, the stairs would give advanced warning of anyone attempting to climb them. She was taking no chances.

'Tell me about working with Jordan,' I asked John as we pulled on our clothes, getting ready for breakfast.

He sighed. 'I can't. I'm still in denial.'

'What?'

'It's a memory I've tried to repress.'

'Why? What happened?'

'I've never felt so inadequate.'

I grabbed his arm and shook it roughly. 'What happened?'

'Well, she was a bit... How can I put it? She was a bit like... Who's that guy who goes around avenging all the evils in the world?'

'Nemesis?' I suggested.

'Who?' he looked puzzled. 'I was thinking of the Silver Surfer. Or was it...?' His brow furrowed as he cast his mind back to his comic book days. 'Who's Nemesis?'

'A Greek concept,' I explained. 'Divine vengeance.'

'Oh! Well, that's good too.'

'What happened?'

'It's difficult to say. I didn't see that much of her.'

'You were her partner!'

'Well, somebody should have explained that to Jordan. I spent a whole week chasing her tail. I'd arrive at places about an hour after she'd left and have to clean up the mess.' He shook his head as he recalled.

'And what did she achieve?'

He whistled in response. 'A lot! You remember a thug called Brian Danvers?'

'Vaguely.' The name was familiar.

'He was a real cowboy; the boss of a nasty group. Armed robbery, drugs, prostitution, you name it, they were into it. But we could never touch him. We convicted his minions every now and then, but never Danvers. He was too careful. We never stopped trying; charged him with various offences over the years but nothing ever stuck.' I nodded. It was a familiar story. 'The second morning... yeah, Tuesday, Jordan told me to drive to his club. I assumed she just wanted to take a look, but when we got there, she hopped out and went in.'

'What about you?'

'I was...' John looked increasingly uneasy. 'I stayed in the car,' he admitted reluctantly.

'Why?'

'She handcuffed me to the steering wheel.'

'What!'

'Yeah,' he smiled. 'She walked into the club, bold as brass. About twenty minutes later, two of his goons *escorted* her off the premises, quite roughly.' He nodded as the vision of a struggling uniformed Jordan flashed through his mind.

'Two days later, Thursday, Danvers walks into the station and makes a voluntary statement, puts his hands up to living off immoral earnings. It was the only conviction we ever got against him.'

I frowned. 'It's a pretty minor charge.'

'It didn't matter,' John explained. 'He got six months. He died in prison.'

'Yeah?'

'He had cancer. He'd never have survived long enough to go to trial. Because he pleaded guilty, it was all over quickly.'

'So, how did she manage it?'

John shrugged. 'I asked her that once. She said she thought it better I didn't know.' I reflected for a few moments, but John wasn't finished. 'And that wasn't all. She was only with us for four weeks, but she cleared up more crime than we normally do in a year.'

'So why'd she move on?'

'I don't really know. Friends in high places, I figured.'

'But she was in Castleton for a month, right?'

'She was in uniform for a month. After that she was spirited into CID.'

By mid-morning John and I were already going stir crazy. The only form of entertainment at the cottage was a TV that was so small it was like watching a play from the most distant seat in a theatre.

When John started moaning about being bored, Jordan told him, 'There are games.'

I rolled my eyes and shook my head, but John appeared interested. 'What have you got?'

'Scrabble,' she replied.

'Yeah, what else?'

She paused to think. 'Just Scrabble.'

He sighed. 'I guess it'll have to be Scrabble, then. Who's playing?'

'You two play. I'd rather read,' I responded quickly and wandered into the front room.

'Are you sure?' asked John with a worried expression.

'Quite sure,' I replied smiling. I exchanged a momentary glance with Jordan, trying to say, "Be gentle with him".

I'd later learn that back in London, the forensic team was still busy. Faced with the unidentified set of prints, they'd eliminated all the police officers present without finding a match.

Garratt was in his office flicking through photos of the house in Engadene Street and reflecting on his conversation with Cathy Pollock. As he worked it through in his mind, something didn't ring true. His tentative thread of logic proceeded like this: Cathy had admitted being in the house and although it had been months before, he would still have expected her fingerprints to be recovered. After all, Arnold wasn't exactly the world's greatest cleaner. So Garratt rang forensics and asked them to double check Cathy's prints to make quite certain. Within minutes, they'd confirmed there was no match.

There was also the matter of the explicit photo. There had to be a reason why Cathy hadn't reported receiving it. She still had a lot of questions to answer.

So, he reasoned, what had happened to Cathy on the last day of term was part of Arnold's established pattern. At least one of his previous victims had received an obscene photo of herself. From that point, Arnold intensified his campaign, yet Cathy had insisted he'd lost interest in her. Why had Cathy escaped his clutches totally unharmed? He rang the duty sergeant to ask him to bring Cathy in for another interview.

She hadn't reported for duty that morning.

When his secretary delivered his morning mail, Garratt was still perplexed. 'I don't think there's anything too pressing this morning,' she told him, laying a pile of internal envelopes on his desk. 'Oh! This was hand-delivered to the front desk.' She passed him a buff A5 envelope with his name hand-written on the front.

He went cold.

'Is everything all right?' she asked, recognising the change in his expression.

He opened a desk drawer and pulled out a pair of latex gloves, clumsily pulling them on over his stubby fingers. Using a sharp letter opener in the shape of a crusader sword, he slit open the envelope. Holding it above the blotter on his desk, he let the contents slide out. It was another postcard, but the subject matter didn't tally with what he was expecting. It pictured an overweight middle-aged woman with a wide bulging neck and an unattractive face. Her right hand stretched out to a naked child who had taken hold of her little finger. Two female bystanders looked on from the left edge of the picture, while two men stood on the right.

Picking the postcard up by its edges, he turned it over and, despite his confusion, the caption confirmed his worst fears. The picture was by Jacob Jordaens and it was entitled 'The Mystic Marriage of St Catherine of Alexandria'. Catherine showed none of the youth and purity of the other saints whose pictures we'd been sent. It was a singularly unattractive image. What concerned Garratt most was not her facial features, but her fate, commemorated every year alongside that of Guy Fawkes.

'Shit!' he exclaimed, picking up the phone. He re-dialled the duty sergeant at Green Park. 'Has Cathy Pollock turned up yet?' he asked.

'No. She's late.'

'What's her address?'

'Hold on.' After some minutes, he came back to the phone. '61 Engadene Street.'

I wouldn't mind betting he groaned at the news, just as I did when I was told. It was just a stone's throw from the house where we'd discovered Celia's body. The middle-aged, puffy-faced man PC Peebles had interviewed on the doorstep the previous day was presumably none other than Lawrence Arnold himself. After he'd abandoned his own home, he hadn't gone far, just up the road. He must have taken great satisfaction watching the police operation from his new hideout.

I think Garratt had a fair idea of what he was going to encounter at number 61. He assembled the assault team again and made sure forensics were ready for another sleepless night.

This was all going on while I was sitting in the cramped front room of the cottage reading a book. I found it impossible to concentrate, skimming whole paragraphs and having to go back and read them again properly. In the kitchen, John and Jordan were still playing Scrabble. I've never heard such a quiet game in my life. Neither player spoke, but occasionally

I could hear the sound of a tile being placed rather heavily on the board. 'That's not a word,' I overheard John say quietly, almost apologetically.

'It is!' Jordan replied with an angry conviction. I shook my head. Maybe Scrabble hadn't been a good idea.

John went very quiet, only to repeat the performance ten minutes later. 'That's not a word!' he insisted.

'It is!' Jordan stressed and John didn't push it.

Abruptly, after an hour, I heard the sound of a chair being pushed back. Jordan appeared in the doorway. 'I'm going to check the grounds. Stay where you are.'

'Allison!' came a hoarse whisper from the kitchen.

'What?'

'Come in here a minute.' I got up and went to the kitchen where surprisingly few words had been laid on the board. There must have been an awful lot of thinking and very little action. I tried not to look at the scoreboard Jordan was meticulously maintaining. 'What's this word, 'ondine'. I put down 'dine' and she comes along and adds ON. What the hell's it mean?'

'It's some kind of Greek water nymph,' I told him.

'You're making that up!'

I shook my head.

'Well, what's this then? Rhea!'

'That depends. You'll have to ask her.'

'What's that supposed to mean?'

'It has more than one meaning. I assume she means the flightless South American bird, but it could also be the wife of Cronus in Greek mythology.'

'Who's Cronus?'

'The father of Zeus. One of the Titans, I think.'

'Titans? One of Jordan's relatives, you mean? Wouldn't that make it a proper noun?'

'Yes, it would. Unless she means the bird.' I studied the board for several minutes before asking, 'Don't you know any words longer than four letters?'

He looked offended. 'How do you know I didn't put down that one?' he asked, pointing towards "menses".

'Just a wild guess,' I answered. 'You might have put down the "men".'

'I did, as it happens.' He looked at the word again. 'Is that a word?'

'Yes.'

'What does it mean?'

'Ask Jordan.'

'No! She might hit me.'

'She's here to protect you, not to attack you.'

He replied with a grunt, unconvinced. 'Have you told her that?'

'I come to praise Caesar, not to bury him!' I added.

'What?' We heard Jordan return through the front door. 'Don't say anything!' he urged.

Jordan re-entered the room smelling of the countryside. She eyed the pair of us suspiciously. 'Don't worry,' I assured her. 'John thought you were cheating.'

'I never said...!' mumbled John as Jordan eyed him with what could pass for hatred in her eyes. John was flustered. 'Well... what does this mean then, rhea?'

'South American bird,' she responded.

'Ah, I thought you might mean the Greek god... Titan! You know... the husband of Cromon.'

'The wife of Cronus!' he heard in stereo.

*

Having discussed events with Garratt and studied the photos in all their gory brutality, I think I can piece together exactly what went on that afternoon in Engadene Street, while we were at the safe house. As the team assembled at number 61, they could all see the crime scene tape still blocking the entrance to the house down the road. A single solitary constable remained on guard duty.

Number 61 was in total darkness. There was no indication that anyone was at home. Garratt stepped up to the front door, pushing the doorbell firmly and slapping on the woodwork with the flat of his hand. 'Police! Open up!' he shouted. After waiting several seconds for a reply, he tried the knob and was surprised when it turned and the door swung open. The layout of the house was identical to Arnold's lair and Garratt allocated his men throughout the house. The forensic team tagged along behind, reluctant to touch anything or open any doors. Garratt strode through to the kitchen, confidently expecting to find Cathy in the basement. As he moved the table and chairs he experienced a feeling of déjà vu. He pulled up the trap door and smelled the air. All that registered was mildew and dampness.

'Sir!' shouted a constable from the doorway. 'I think you'd better get upstairs.'

Garratt looked at the white-suited forensic technician, who shrugged. Together they made their way upstairs towards an open door. Standing on the threshold of the room, Garratt drew in his breath sharply. 'Jesus Christ!' The day before he had interviewed this girl. Today, she was dead.

'Wow!' muttered the technician in what could almost have been admiration. Garratt watched as he approached the hideous spectacle and bent down to see more clearly.

Absentmindedly, he pulled on a pair of gloves and studied the construction of the device. 'This is extraordinary!' he whispered.

'It's a Catherine wheel,' stated Garratt sullenly.

Cathy Pollock's body was stretched out around the curved edge of a laminated semicircle. The wheel was constructed of wooden floorboards. The top was flat along its diameter and rested almost horizontally. Each board was a few inches shorter at each end than the one above, creating the illusion of a semicircle with a radius of about three feet. Her back was attached to the wheel by several leather straps.

Even from a distance, Garratt could see that her arms and legs followed the contours of the wheel with unnatural accuracy, clearly broken as she was tied. She was resting beneath the wheel, her stomach against the floor, its enormous weight compressing her body. Her head hung down almost allowing her forehead to touch the floor. On top of the carpet along the path of the wheel, like a track of a train, lay another floorboard. Nails had been hammered through from the bottom and their sharp spikes projected above its surface by about two inches. She had been impaled upon them as the wheel rotated. In addition, the small section of the wheel's circumference visible where her head drooped forward was also complete with protruding nails. They only projected about an inch, insufficient to cause death, but enough to cause agony. Cathy's blood had pooled and was beginning to congeal around the base, soaking the carpet.

Back in the car, Garratt used the radio to place a call to the CID office to break the news. He also asked a sergeant to check the records of the house-to-house enquiries the previous day, to see whether anyone had been at home at number

61. He felt a sudden chill as it dawned on him that Arnold himself may well have been questioned.

So where was he now?

Desperate enquiries were started to discover whether Cathy could have known the location of the safe house, in which case Arnold would know it too. The police came to the correct conclusion that Cathy hadn't known. It didn't matter. Arnold was already travelling west. One young secretary, who was subsequently dismissed, had felt adrift without her word processor. No matter how hard she looked, she couldn't find the delete key or the spell-checker on the typewriter. No problem: she'd quickly typed up an inventory of supplies and a delivery address for the safe house on her computer, printed it, then equally quickly deleted it. She didn't realise that deleted files remained on the disk until they were overwritten.

Chapter 15

After nearly two hours, John stormed out of the kitchen and sat down next to me, breathing heavily.

'I assume from your demeanour you didn't win?' I remarked casually.

John snorted. 'She doesn't like me!' he whispered, making sure Jordan couldn't overhear.

'Now, why would you think that?' I asked sarcastically.

'Have you seen the way she looks at me? Like I'm dirt or something.'

'She's like that with everyone, John,' I explained.

'She's not like it with you,' he pointed out. 'I think she sees me as a rival for your affections,' he said with a nod of his head.

'Don't be absurd!'

'I'm going to find a dictionary. I'll prove she was cheating.'

I shook my head and stood up. In the kitchen, Jordan looked self-satisfied, bordering on the smug, as she sat at the table nuzzling a cup of purple tea. She pulled out a pink cardboard folder from her overnight bag. Leafing through the pages, she began to read, arranging a set of crime scene photos in a semicircle.

I stood at the sink, from where I could see little of the photos carefully arranged on the table. Jordan remained a picture of concentration flicking through a bundle of notes. 'What's that?' I asked.

'The Chinese diplomat,' she replied.

'Can I?' I asked drawing closer.

Jordan shrugged.

I recognised the pictures. They were of the girl who was found in Green Park. No doubt Jordan also had the post-mortem photos I'd "acquired" for her. 'Ah! The China Doll. Is it true she was stuf...?' I stopped myself abruptly. I could feel Jordan's penetrating glare on my face. 'I'm not supposed to know about that, am I?' I asked guiltily.

Jordan shook her head.

The fact that the child had been stuffed and her skin preserved in a natural, flexible state, was a feature that had been successfully concealed from the press, but the Force's grapevine was capable of disseminating information at an alarming rate.

I sighed. 'You know Cathy Pollock at Green Park? She got you the post-mortem photos.' I enquired, feeling the need to provide an explanation.

'I met her.'

'I went to college with her.'

Jordan nodded. WPC Pollock had been one of the first on the scene when the dead girl's body was discovered.

'Sorry,' I mumbled.

Jordan shrugged. 'People talk.'

'Most people!' I corrected staring at her.

Jordan eyed me with a trace of suspicion, her mouth twitching as though ready to break into a smile. But she regained control and her face once again became a mask that displayed no emotion.

'How did you become involved?' I asked, surprised.

'I... was asked to take a look.'

I knew that wasn't true! 'I thought you were...'

'Suspended?'

'I was going to say I thought you were a bodyguard.'

'I do a little police work in my spare time.'

I nodded, not sure if she was being sarcastic. 'But why you?'

Jordan sighed. She had been through this routine many times before. 'I'm a detective, right?' she looked up for some sign of recognition. 'I get assigned cases where they think I may be able to help.'

I was silent for some moments. 'So, it's right, is it? She was stu...'

'Yes!' Jordan broke in sharply. 'She was stuffed!'

'So what's your next step? Why Beijing?'

She drew a long, tortured breath. 'The children come from China,' she replied as if that were explanation enough.

'Children plural?'

'Yes.'

'And?' I prompted.

'And I speak Mandarin.'

'You do?'

'Yes.'

'Why?'

'My grandparents are multilingual.'

'Really?'

'Yes.'

I thought for a few minutes. Jordan had family! I hadn't considered the possibility before. 'What sort of person would stuff a child and preserve her body?'

'Probably the same kind that kills women in the manner of Roman and medieval martyred saints.'

'I don't understand, but I wouldn't mind sitting in on the interview.'

'What interview?'

'With Arnold.'

Jordan just grunted.

'What?'

'We have to catch him first.'

'Well?'

She looked at me with a sad shake of the head.

'Don't look at me as if I'm stupid!'

Jordan looked visibly shocked, almost apologetic. 'No! I *know* you're not stupid, but you're underestimating your opponent.'

'You don't think we'll catch him?'

She shrugged.

'Talk to me!'

Instead of talking, she sighed and bent to withdraw more documents from her bag. She laid out the three photos of Lawrence Arnold: the ID photo from FlexTech and the two images taken in the alley near my flat. Jordan just sat and looked at the three disparate images.

'Okay, so he has a talent for disguise.'

'And an unlimited number of IDs,' Jordan added.

I sat back, accepting the point. 'So?'

'Maybe he doesn't *want* to be caught.'

'What do you mean?'

She took a deep breath. 'Why is he doing this?'

'I have no idea.'

'No, but he does. Sooner or later, he's going to want everyone else to know. He'll want recognition. His justification will be ready and he'll want to take credit.'

'So, he'll want to be caught.'

'At some point.'

'Maybe he'll come here,' I suggested.

'You'd better hope he doesn't!' she said sharply.

'Why?'

Jordan looked at me to check whether I was joking. Actually, I wasn't. 'Because we wouldn't stand a chance.'

'Why? You're both armed.'

Jordan took a moment to think. 'We're not here to defend you. We're here to hide you. What do you think would happen if Arnold finds out where you are and comes after you?'

I considered the problem and remained silent.

'One grenade through the window and we're all outside. Then he can pick us off one by one. Or a stun grenade, or a fire. There's only so much two people can do. We should have bulletproof glass and a whole squad surrounding the place.' She shrugged.

'Right,' I pondered.

'I'll do everything I can, but don't expect miracles. If he finds us, people will die.'

She had an uncanny knack of evaluating situations and accurately predicting the outcome. 'I guess we better hope he doesn't find out where we are.'

'But people talk, don't they?'

Jordan wasn't often pessimistic. On the rare occasions she was, there was usually good reason.

Garratt told me he spent the remainder of the morning reviewing certain books recovered from Engadene Street: *A History of Torture*, *Curious Punishments of Bygone Days*, *The History of the Inquisition* and *History of Flagellation Among Different Nations*. I should imagine they made for pretty uncomfortable reading. I later flicked through them and had to wonder what sort of person wrote books of that nature and, more importantly, who read them.

Having spoken briefly with PC Peebles, Garratt was stopped short by the arrival of the post-mortem report on Celia Potter. Peebles confirmed that he'd spoken with the occupant of number 61, a Colin Reece. His name was checked against a valid driver's licence.

Celia's cause of death was beheading. There were pages of physical injuries inflicted ante-mortem, everything from suppurating lacerations to cigarette burns. A more detailed list of her injuries was still in preparation. Apparently, her orifices had been widely dilated.

What about the rats? Well, the rats were definitely applied post-mortem. The exit wounds where the rats had burrowed free showed a lack of blood: evidence that the circulatory system had already ceased. They found no semen on the body or inside. The only traces of semen were on the floor of the torture chamber and in the upstairs bedroom.

So, depending on your definition, she hadn't necessarily been sexually abused. However, they got a positive match on the ovary discovered in my locker. It was Celia's. It had been removed prior to death and none too carefully. Whatever else Lawrence Arnold might be, he was no surgeon.

All these details would be communicated to Jordan and me later, after the events of that night. We were still sitting around the farmhouse, bored out of our minds and arguing over who would do the cooking. John finally decided he wasn't hungry and stormed off to take a shower. I took the opportunity to engage Jordan in conversation. I'd decided it was time I knew something about her.

I looked across the kitchen table at her. As usual, she was

concentrating on another file, something to do with her efforts in Rotterdam. 'Tell me about Brian Danvers,' I suggested.

She snorted without looking up.

'Jordan!'

Carefully, she replaced the sheet squarely on top of the pile, nudging it perfectly into line with her fingertips. 'He was scum.'

'So how did you do it?'

Jordan took a long breath. 'I identified his weakness.'

'Which was?'

'His family,' she admitted reluctantly. 'He had two teenage sons.'

Unpleasant thoughts flitted through my mind. 'And?'

'They had misguided notions of following in their father's footsteps, only they weren't quite as careful,' she informed me.

'So you had something on them?'

'Oh, yeah.'

'And you *traded* it with their father?'

After a minor hesitation, she responded, 'Something like that.'

I eyed Jordan with suspicion. 'So Danvers gives himself up and the children go free.'

Jordan had the decency to look a little sheepish. 'After we had Danvers' confession, I went after the kids.'

'And?'

'They got twelve years.'

'Twelve years! What for?'

Jordan thought for a moment. 'Perpetuating the family line,' she replied with a wry smile.

I thought it unlikely that I'd get any more information and made a mental note to ask John when we were alone. 'So, what did you make of John, your *partner*?' I asked innocently.

Jordan's eyes didn't waver from her notes. 'I didn't see a lot of him.'

'Yes, he told me he had trouble keeping up with you.' I remained silent for a while, then asked, 'And now? What do you make of him now?'

With a sigh, she disengaged her eyes and sat back in her chair. 'Are you looking for my approval?'

I shrugged, 'Maybe. What do you think?'

Jordan shrugged.

'Tell me!'

Silence.

'You think I made a mistake?'

Jordan shrugged again.

'Look, Jordan, I know conversation isn't your favourite pastime, but would it kill you to make an effort?' I sat back and crossed my arms. Now I was sulking. 'Spit it out, for Christ's sake, Jordan! What's up with you? You worried about hurting my feelings?'

'Yes.'

'Oh.' I felt deflated.

'Look, John's a decent guy. He's just shallow. You're worth more than that.' She held out her hands as though everything was now crystal clear.

'How do you know what I'm like?'

'I'm a good judge of character.'

'Really?' I nodded appreciatively. 'So I'm not shallow. What am I?'

Jordan thought for a few moments before admitting, 'I like you.'

I smiled. 'That's good Jordan, but...' I shrugged hopelessly. Evidently the gesture was infectious. 'Take a look at me. I'm not exactly in a position to be fussy.'

Jordan looked until she was satisfied, then she placed a reassuring hand on my shoulder. 'Yes, you are,' she told me. With a quick shake of her head, she went on, 'So, you and John, you're...?'

'Yeah, but it's only been a few days.'

I watched her digest the news. It was nothing she didn't already know; perhaps she just needed to hear it from me. Her face was impassive, but I could almost sense her thoughts racing. I wondered what she was thinking as her eyes concentrated on a dirty mark on the tabletop. Finally, she looked up. 'Is he what you want?'

I shrugged. 'I don't know. That's part of the fun, finding out.' I took a deep breath. 'You have someone?'

'No, I...'

'I'm not like you, Jordan. I don't want to be on my own.'

Jordan descended into contemplation, nodding gently to herself.

'I mean, what made you this way in the first place?' I asked. 'You have some great childhood trauma?'

Abruptly, she stood, her face hardening and every muscle stiffening. 'I have to check the perimeter.'

I stood and blocked Jordan's path to the door. When she attempted to skirt around me, I grabbed both her arms. 'Tell me,' I urged.

Staring straight ahead and ignoring my presence, she quietly responded, 'My parents died when I was nine.'

'How?' I asked gently.

'Because of me,' she answered and, taking advantage of my momentary shock, pulled her arms free and walked through the door.

Never for a moment did I think she was talking literally. Despite being enthusiastic in her use of deadly weapons, I figured it was a trait that developed as she got older. Nine is a pretty tender age. Nine-year-olds don't necessarily see the bigger picture. What might have seemed her responsibility at the time, could well have been totally beyond her control. Whatever happened, it was obvious she still held herself responsible for her parents' deaths.

I was told it took hours before Cathy Pollock's body could be removed from the scene. When it arrived at the morgue, a preliminary examination was immediately undertaken. The pathologist discovered numerous superficial wounds all over her body. Her back was a mass of scar tissue and her arms and legs were covered with healed lacerations and burns. Her body showed evidence of the familiar dilations.

In line with normal procedure, Cathy's fingerprints were taken from the body. They were then compared to those on file. They didn't match. Forensics quickly confirmed that the second unidentified set of prints recovered from the first house on Engadene Street matched those from Cathy's body. She'd been a regular visitor and had been present during Celia's ordeal. Her prints were etched into Celia's blood in the basement room.

The fingerprint record had been switched. Although those in her physical personnel file matched those of her corpse, the computer records had been changed. It was a neat trick and afforded Arnold the luxury of a significant head start. If we'd identified Cathy's presence in the original house, we would have been knocking on the door of number 61 much sooner. Once again, Arnold's computer trickery had gained him precious hours.

John and I were talking while Jordan was conducting one of her regular patrols around the perimeter. He was filling me in on some of the missing details.

'And you know what she did then?' John asked, chuckling to himself.

I cleared my throat loudly, very loudly. He didn't get the hint.

'She told him...' Suddenly, John turned his head and looked directly into Jordan's fuming face.

'Don't stop on my account,' she told him through gritted teeth.

'No! It was just... Somebody else, actually... Yes, two other people,' he blurted through his embarrassment.

Jordan didn't say anything and concentrated on her file.

'I'm hungry!' John announced to no-one in particular as the night drew in. 'What is there to eat?'

Jordan didn't look up from her file. After a long sigh I stood up. 'Why don't we take a look.' Together we walked across the kitchen and pulled open the fridge door. A brief scan revealed the parlous state of our provisions. 'Eggs,' I told him.

'I had eggs for breakfast.'

'And lunch,' I reminded him. 'There's some cheese.'

John wasn't impressed. 'If Arnold doesn't kill us, the cholesterol will.' I ignored him. Then he had an idea. 'Couldn't we get Jordan to shoot one of those bloody chickens?'

'I don't think so.' After deciding there was enough bread left, I suggested, 'Cheese on toast?'

'Brilliant! Got any ketchup?'

'No.'

'Jordan,' I called. 'Do you want some cheese on toast?'

'Yeah,' she said without enthusiasm.

'Maybe you could give us a hand?' John suggested.

Her expression didn't change. 'How many hands does it take to toast a slice of bread?'

'I think four's probably enough,' I informed them both diplomatically.

'I have to check the perimeter,' Jordan told them, despite the fact she'd only just sat down.

'That's convenient!' responded John sarcastically. She turned back to confront him, her face a picture of hostility. 'Do you ever wish you'd been born a man, Jordan?' he asked.

'No,' she responded calmly. 'Do you?'

John watched her departing back with a puzzled expression on his face. When he turned to me, I quickly wiped the smirk from my face. 'I told you she doesn't like me.'

'Perhaps if you'd stop behaving like a child?'

'It's her fault! She's always so hostile. I bet she hasn't got any friends.'

I thought for a few moments before admitting, 'She has one. Besides, she has things on her mind at the moment: the suspension...'

'Don't worry,' John reassured me. 'She'll come out smelling of roses again. She always does.'

I shook my head wearily. 'I think she's in real trouble. Too many people want her head.'

'Really? I thought she was fireproof.'

'Not this time.' I thought for some time, slicing cheese, before shaking my head. 'I asked her about Danvers.'

'That was brave.'

'She said she put his sons away too.'

John thought back across the span of several years. 'That's right!'

'What was that for?' I asked.

'Um, they abducted a schoolgirl, about fourteen. Then they took turns with her.'

'Oh!' No wonder she broke her promise.

'There was other stuff too but Jordan didn't follow it up.'

'Like what?'

'They did a sub-post office, beat up the post master. Got away with a couple of grand. Oh, and there was something about a Securicor van. They didn't get the money but one of the guards was injured.'

'But she didn't pursue those?'

'No.'

I found my admiration for Jordan growing exponentially. She'd been prepared to overlook a spot of robbery to convict their father, but not the rape of a schoolgirl. 'What do you know about her parents?' I asked.

'Nothing. Has she got any?'

That evening, we'd received a call from Garratt to check that everything was okay. We moaned a little about the food and the entertainment, but quite rightly, he informed us that it wasn't supposed to be a holiday camp. He brought us up to date with all the developments in London, not going into great detail, but telling us enough to make us queasy. He also informed us that the beheaded corpse found so long ago in Cumbria had been tentatively identified as Susanna Gold.

Somehow, he'd managed to fit in a second interview with Arnold's father: this time at the station. When Anthony Arnold had been informed of Susanna's identity, he provided an instant response hinted at by Father Williams in Rome: 'Saint Susanna, died circa 295, Cumae, death by beheading'. The passage of time clearly hadn't dimmed his memory. When informed that her death remained an open case, he denied that his son could be involved. 'Why would he kill Susanna? It was years later,' he pointed out.

'Maybe someone planted the idea in his head,' Garratt suggested.

'Woolcraft, you mean?' came the instant reply.

As the night turned black, Jordan was clearly uneasy. She tried her best to conceal it, but every chiselled feature of her face twitched with disquiet. She took exaggerated care ensuring that every square inch of each window was obscured by curtain, like a blackout. I believe she'd deduced that that night would be Arnold's first and best opportunity to attack. We'd been safe the previous night because we hadn't arrived until the early hours. He simply wouldn't have had time to put together a viable strategy. Now she was counting the hours, trying to figure out where he would strike.

'What's the matter, Jordan?' I asked. Her constant fidgeting was unnerving us all.

'Nothing!' she replied emphatically, checking the curtains.

'Are you planning to sleep on the landing again tonight?' John asked.

Jordan said nothing. I think she assumed that we'd be sleeping together and one part of her would have been relieved: it was easier to patrol a single room. Another part of her would have been anxious.

'You need rest,' I told her.

Jordan nodded weakly and looked at John with distaste. Maybe she simply couldn't fathom what I saw in him, the concept of our relationship. She thought him weak and ignorant, not a suitable partner. She later admitted that he possessed a superficial attractiveness, but broadcast his inadequacies whenever he opened his mouth.

'Bed,' Jordan said abruptly.

'What?' replied John, but a single glance from her silenced any potential dispute.

'Come on,' I urged taking hold of his arm.

As we passed Jordan, I smiled and tried to reassure her, brushing my hand to her bare arm. Jordan looked down in confusion. We prepared for bed and Jordan took up position at the foot of the stairs, offering us a little privacy. Later on, we heard her move up to the corridor and settle outside the room.

We could hear all the noises of the house. Later, the front door opened as Michael stepped inside. 'All clear?' asked Jordan.

'Quiet as a graveyard.' I could almost feel Jordan's contemptuous glare. 'Ease up, Lassiter,' he went on. 'Get some sleep.'

She would rest whilst remaining on her guard, poised to strike. The balls of her feet rested on the polished floor prepared to push off in any direction.

Chapter 16

'Tell me what happened at the farmhouse,' Jeffries suggested. He, Ramsden and Garratt had been asking me the same question ever since that fateful night. It might surprise you to hear that I'd managed to avoid talking about it to anyone. I hadn't even given a formal statement. I wouldn't have got away with it for so long, but events quickly overtook us all. It wouldn't be long before Jordan and I were desperately trying to keep one step ahead of the police, just like Arnold.

So, John and I had gone to bed. Jordan was sitting outside the door. Michael was on duty and periodically performed a circuit of the grounds making sure the coast was clear. The farmhouse itself was in complete darkness. No-one had slept well the previous night and exhaustion quickly overcame us. John and I both fell asleep.

At about two o'clock we were disturbed. We were both instantly alert and on our guard. Through the gloom we could just about make out Jordan standing in the doorway.

'Wake up!' she hissed urgently.

'What?'

'Get up! We have company.'

We responded with groans.

'Don't turn on the light!'

With that, she was gone. We listened as she made her way downstairs, pausing to scan the surroundings from the window on the landing. Everything appeared quiet. It was at this stage that she'd pulled out her mobile phone and dialled her liaison, requesting immediate backup. We were under attack and the clock was now ticking. Being located in the middle of nowhere had its drawbacks. Help would take at least fifteen minutes to arrive, but we were aware it could take longer. Had Jordan been on her own, she would have been outside taking her chances one on one, confident that she could overcome any adversary. However, as long as we stayed in the house, so did she.

It was then that she'd noticed something on the mat just inside the front door. Arnold had made another characteristic delivery. I was only told of this development the following day. The house was in complete darkness and when she picked it up, she couldn't make out the details. Had we known what it depicted, had we been forewarned, I still don't think we could have done anything differently.

We threw on some clothes and raced downstairs to join Jordan.

'Quiet!' she hissed. She didn't want us to reveal our position. We crouched beside her as she knelt by the window, periodically lifting the curtain marginally to see out. 'Get away!' she ordered, pushing John roughly. 'Over by the door,' she pointed. 'Now!' We crept across the floor on all fours until we were against the wall, nestling in the shelter of the open door. Jordan was staring out of the window, her eyes attuned to the darkness. I don't think she saw anything. She let the curtain drop and turned towards us. 'Sit!' she ordered.

Shocked, we sat down. John put his arm around my shoulder and whispered, 'It'll be all right.'

Jordan gave him an incredulous glance and shook her head.

'Where's Michael?' I asked.

Jordan shrugged.

'What are we going to do?'

'Sit tight.'

'Have you called for backup?' asked John.

After a condescending snort, she replied firmly, 'Yes!'

'How long will they be?'

'As long as it takes.'

'But, what...'

'Quiet!' she insisted. She wanted to think. She was trying to put herself in the mind of our pursuer. What would he do? It was obvious he would want us out of the house. He couldn't risk coming in while she was armed. A full-frontal assault on the door was doomed to failure. She would pick him off as he entered. He had to disable her and take possession of the gun. She had to assume he already had Michael's weapon.

Then she figured it out.

'Keep your heads down!' she whispered hoarsely and made her way towards the kitchen. That was where he would strike.

She was standing no more than a yard from the door when we heard the window shatter. There followed a deep 'whumf' and a blinding orange light blew her off her feet. As she was propelled backwards, she demolished the coffee table and her gun flew from her hand. As she tried to pull herself upright, she shook her head, stunned. Her skin was singed and I was pretty sure she no longer had any eyebrows or lashes. She exercised her jaw from side to side, trying to regain her senses, but her skin must have hurt.

I was first to my feet, pushing the kitchen door closed and confining the flames behind a stout hardwood barrier.

'Gun!' said Jordan, holding out her hand, still dazed.

John leapt to his feet and fetched it. She studied the heavy metal, checking the clip and ensuring it was still in working order. She tried to clear her head. She had to think. What now? She was breathing very heavily.

'Take the gun. I'm going out,' Jordan told John, holding out the weapon. 'Give me your jacket.'

He took the gun in his hand, shaking his head. The noise of the flames consuming the kitchen was growing louder. Wisps of black smoke had begun to emerge from beneath the door. I did my best to seal the gap with cushions.

'Wait!' I said. 'What are you planning to do?'

Apparently Jordan thought her strategy was quite clear. As far as she was concerned, there was only one thing she could do. She had to go outside and bring him down. If we stayed where we were, there would be another assault. That's if we didn't succumb to smoke inhalation first. Someone had to go out and stop him. 'I'm going to kill him,' she said plainly.

'Then you'll need the gun.'

'No. Protect yourselves.'

'Jordan,' I urged. 'If you kill him we won't need to protect ourselves and you're not going to kill him unless you take the gun.'

Jordan worked through the options. She was quite capable of taking Arnold with her bare hands, but even she had to admit that with a gun she'd have a better chance. She breathed out heavily, considering. Finally, she took the gun out of John's hand and waited for his black jacket. 'Don't leave unless you have to,' she told us as she pulled it on. She didn't want us outside at all, but the noise of the fire was a warning that we didn't have long.

Jordan's senses were gradually returning after her fall,

but her chest must have ached. She tried not to show it. With a curt nod, she disappeared towards the back of the house.

If Arnold thought she'd exit by the front door, then he'd made a serious mistake. She opened a rear window as noiselessly as she could, resting her sneakers on the windowsill. 'Lock the window!' she hissed back, and by the time I approached all I could see was her back disappearing into the night. I heard no crunch of gravel. She must have bounded right over the path and onto the grass.

We tried everything to prevent smoke entering the room. We plugged the gaps around the kitchen door with damp towels and cushions, but we were fighting a losing battle. The door was over a hundred years old. It was dry as tinder and smoke was billowing into the room around its edges. We only had a few minutes before the smoke would overcome us.

We wrapped damp cloths around our faces in a futile attempt to filter the poisonous air. The roaring flames from behind the kitchen door prevented us from hearing anything that was going on outside. Jordan was fighting for our lives and we had no idea how she was getting on. Occasional mild explosions from the kitchen made us jump as we mistook them for gunshots. We tried to cling close to the floor to avoid the worst of the acrid smoke. Ultimately, it was hopeless. I felt myself growing dizzy as the oxygen became thinner.

'Allison!' shouted John, struggling to make himself heard above the inferno. Briefly, I jolted myself back to consciousness. The kitchen door was smouldering and red sparks were threatening to turn to flames. The room was full of dense smoke. I couldn't see the window anymore.

I'd temporarily lost consciousness lying on the floor, still resting obediently beside the door. I don't know how long I was out of it, but it could only have been moments. My position offered little protection. I still had a damp teatowel wrapped around my head. I felt lightheaded as John shook my shoulder. When he received no response, he went to the front door and drew back the bolt. Taking the handle, he pulled it inwards ready to inhale the fresh air that would give him the strength to carry me to safety. Of course, Jordan had locked it.

Like me, John had no idea what was going on outside, but he realised that if we remained inside, we'd both die. Our hopes were pinned on Jordan and despite everything, we still had enormous faith in her.

The door key was on the mantelpiece, but visibility in the room was virtually zero. I was flitting in and out of consciousness. John passed his hands along the wooden shelf, bumping into ornaments and sending them flying. The keys were on a small plastic ring and he worked around the central clock listening desperately for the chink of metal. There they were! He almost knocked them from the shelf in his excitement. He descended into a trough of guttural coughing, bending double with the effort. He tightened the towel around his head, sick with the smoke.

John took hold of me around the waist and dragged me along the floor. He struggled to find the lock with his fingers. As I lay there unable to control my limbs, I could feel the heat emanating from the kitchen door. He finally located the keyhole and with shaking hands, attempted to insert the key. It stubbornly refused to enter the keyhole, the tip skidding on the escutcheon leaving scratches in the brass plate.

Finally, he forced the key home and turned it with what little strength he had left. He grasped the handle and pulled open the door.

He grabbed hold of me, dragged me over the gravel path and dropped me unceremoniously onto the grass. He checked to ensure that I was breathing but even as he looked down, my eyes opened in response to the clean air. Finally, we were free from the toxic smoke.

All of our hopes now rested on Jordan. There was still no sign of our back-up arriving. We just had to pray that somehow she'd managed to disable him. I looked up at John. He was bent double, but at least his wracking cough had stopped.

We both looked sharply towards the garden as we heard muted footsteps approaching.

Jeffries continued to stare at me, just as he had throughout my sullen monologue. There was no sympathy to be found on his expressionless face. He was obviously aware of the subsequent events, but was able to view them with a calm detachment. I didn't have that luxury.

What happened in the next few minutes would be one of those defining points in my life. I would look back on events, endlessly replaying them in my mind, trying to fashion a different outcome. As Jordan told me, 'Not every question has an answer.' I still haven't been able to work out a chain of events that would have ended happily for any of those concerned. I wasn't about to tell Jeffries *all* the details. I was too ashamed for that. I'd give him the bare bones and he'd just have to be satisfied.

As far as Jordan's role in the unfolding events went, I

can recount her actions accurately. I'd read and reread her statement. She did all she could. The situation was already hopeless by the time she leapt out of the window, ignoring the pain from a broken rib. Michael was unconscious, seated in the barn, his weapon in Arnold's possession. He'd been taken out of the game without so much as a struggle. Jordan wouldn't prove so easy.

From the window ledge, Jordan alighted on the grass and dashed towards the shrubbery. The trees were further away and the waist-high shrubs would afford her an element of cover. Her long legs consumed the distance quickly, her feet barely touching the ground. For a large girl she was amazingly light on her feet.

She believed that Arnold had taken up position at the front of the house, probably behind the laurel hedge. She intended to skirt the area and come up on him from behind. But time was a major factor. If she didn't act quickly, John and I would have to abandon the house or risk asphyxiation. She eyed the line of trees, wishing she had the time to take refuge there and slowly work her way around. She dismissed the idea and dropped onto her stomach.

Her ability to crawl must have been impaired by the pain from her chest. Much as she tried to ignore it, it wouldn't go away and forced her to take short breaks. She made her way along the side of the house no more than a stone's throw from the brickwork. Her adversary would be positioned at a greater distance. She wouldn't be able to take him from behind. She had to rely on surprise alone.

Counting the elapsing minutes in her head, she forced herself onward until she was level with the front corner of the house. She scanned the terrain: the trees in the distance, shrubbery closer in and a single tree trunk. She strained her eyes, coaxing her pupils wider to invite more of an image onto her retina. She noticed something sticking up above a tree stump: something thin and perfectly straight. It reminded her of a rifle barrel.

She was confident she'd identified the target. If she was wrong, she would pay the price. Taking a deep breath, she moved forward, gun clutched in her right hand. As she moved, she planned her strategy. How close could she get without disturbing him? He would be expecting her and watching for any movement. At a distance in the long grass, she could evade detection, but as she closed in she could reveal herself.

She skirted the area, moving further away from the house adjacent to the tree stump. To get a clear shot she would have to be to the side of him: the stump would provide cover from the front. And she needed to surprise him. She could remain on her stomach, but she would need to assume a shooting posture.

Agonisingly, she moved around, trying not to think of what was happening in the house. She was closing in on him. Nearly close enough. She stopped and brought both hands onto the gun. Her marksmanship was excellent. Raising her arms slightly, she took careful aim and fired two shots.

He'd heard her!

Moments before her first shot rang out, he scrambled to one side, but she thought she'd hit him. She didn't know where she hit him or whether the shot was fatal, but she was reasonably sure at least one of the bullets had found its target. She remained silent, listening. He made no noise. He'd fallen lengthways and the stump concealed his body. A single leather-booted foot poked out around its side.

Hesitantly, Jordan approached, raising herself to a crouch. She didn't have the time she needed to take precautions. She had to reach him and make sure he was dead. She watched the boot to ensure he didn't move. Then she saw movement! No more than a twitch or an involuntary muscle spasm, but the boot definitely moved. She hoped it was the result of Arnold writhing in pain or in his final death throes. She had to move further around until his body was in sight.

As she got closer, she held her breath. She stood upright and attempted to see over the top of the waist-high stump, her gun trained on the position where she imagined his body lay.

Then she noticed something.

Her eyes had been so focused on his boot that she'd failed to notice the rifle barrel had disappeared. Moments earlier it had stood erect like a flagpole sticking out of the summit of the stump.

She approached with even greater caution, her gun clutched in both hands. Her aim didn't waver. Never did it leave the area surrounding that boot. That single boot was all she had to show that he'd been there, and was still lying there motionless.

Closer now, twenty yards. She cursed the noise of the fire as she listened for any sign of motion. Then she felt momentarily guilty as she remembered us inside. The air supply would be decreasing every minute as the noxious fumes filled the room. She had to press on.

She was taking longer strides, narrowing the gap. She took a stride to the side, attempting to see around the stump. This was it. All her years of training would boil down to nothing if things didn't pan out over the next few seconds.

She was close now. Still she heard nothing. The boot hadn't moved. She *had* hit him. Another giant stride and her finger twitched on the trigger.

Something moved in her peripheral vision. What?

The other side of the stump!

She looked in alarm as the rifle barrel emerged, pointing directly at her. Her mouth dropped open in surprise.

Then she could see his head. Lagging marginally, her arms followed her line of sight, bringing the gun around.

Too late!

Something struck her squarely in the chest. Slowly, she looked down and saw an extraordinary translucent cylinder protruding from her ribcage with a pretty red tail fluttering in the breeze. She let off a shot but her body was already betraying her. She fell to her knees, the drug flooding her system. She toppled over, her nose making a shallow indentation in the soft ground.

'Go on,' Jeffries prompted.

I was left with another decision to take: exactly what to tell him. I sure as hell wasn't about to describe my full role in the proceedings.

John and I were both on the grass, coughing from smoke damaged lungs and trying desperately to regain our senses.

'Well, well! There's never a policeman around when you need one, is there?' came a voice from the shadows.

We looked up at our worst fear. Lawrence Arnold was striding towards us with a gun in one hand, another tucked into his belt, and a scimitar in his other hand.

'How are we all?' Arnold asked politely, approaching us

menacingly. The flames of the fire flickered, illuminating his face and casting eerie shadows.

John didn't respond.

Arnold nudged me painfully with his foot. 'Get up! We don't have long.'

I struggled to my knees, still gasping for air.

Arnold extracted a length of cord from his jacket pocket and handed it to me. 'Tie your friend's hands in front of him. And do it tightly!'

I looked at the gun and then noticed the sword. So that was where it was! I'd searched for it at his home but he'd kept it with him like a talisman. I looked at it with fear in my eyes. 'No!' I told him, shaking my head.

Arnold pointed the gun at John's right calf and fired. John collapsed in pain, a spray of blood discolouring the grass. I stared in horror. 'The next one will take his head off. Now, tie his hands.' Reluctantly, watching Arnold all the while, I began to tie John's hands. 'Tighter!' Arnold screamed.

I did as he requested. 'Where's Jordan?' I asked.

'Jordan's alive.' He tested the strength of my knots. They were impressively tight if I say so myself. 'Kneel!' he instructed, the gun never leaving John's head. John struggled to his knees, wincing from the pain of his right leg.

'You!' He nudged me with the point of the sword. 'Stand up!'

I inhaled deeply. I was still dizzy, but I stood unsteadily.

'Step back!' he instructed me and I obeyed until I was no longer within reaching distance. 'You!' he kicked John hard on his damaged leg. He cried like a wounded animal. 'Put your hands on the ground with your head horizontal.' John did as he was told. Then Arnold pulled back John's shirt collar exposing his neck to the sword. Arnold lay the blade neatly along the exposed flesh, vertebrae visible through the tight skin. He took hold of the hilt in his right hand, the gun in his left pointed directly at my chest. A drop of blood formed on John's neck where the sharp blade sliced through the flesh. 'Now,' Arnold said with a smirk, looking at me. 'Dance, Salome!'

My mouth dropped open in horror, my head shaking. Then it all became clear. Saint John. John the Baptist. Arnold wasn't after me at all! He never had been. He was after John and he was about to play out the tableau of his beheading, with me playing the part of Salome.

'Dance!' he cried with glee, a smile transforming his face into an image of evil.

I continued to shake my head from side to side. 'No,' I said quietly.

Arnold lifted the blade to the height of his shoulders, preparing to strike. He cocked the gun, still pointing directly at my chest. 'I don't want to kill you,' he explained. 'You're my witness.'

My heart was pumping so fast I could barely register its beats. I was too far away to take on Arnold and any movement would result in a bullet. Still I refused. 'No.'

From nowhere, almost silently, Jordan appeared between Arnold and me. Her head was low and she appeared weary and slow-witted. Every motion was a triumph of determination.

'Wow! How'd you do that?' asked Arnold, his eyebrows raised in appreciation. 'They use these at wildlife parks.'

Jordan stared at him.

'You always were... a marvel!' Arnold shook his head

in admiration, before evidently remembering himself. He cleared his throat noisily before continuing. 'Tidy yourself up Jordan, for Christ's sake!' He reached towards her and took hold of the red-tailed dart, pulling it roughly from her chest. She didn't flinch. A small circle of blood formed around the puncture wound.

As Arnold studied the dart, examining the mechanism and checking that the full dose of tranquilliser had entered Jordan's system, she struck with a round-armed right hook, landing squarely on his jaw. She used every ounce of her remaining strength, but it was a weak swing.

'Ow!' cried Arnold, more in shock than pain. 'That was surprisingly painful considering the state you're in.' His voice mirrored his respect.

In a slurred voice, Jordan informed him, 'I can still kill you.'

Arnold shook his head. 'Now, that wouldn't be a good idea. I wouldn't even try it. I want to protect you, not to hurt you.' I watched as Arnold moved the sword away from John and pointed it directly at Jordan.

Jordan took another exaggerated swing at him, but this time he was prepared and dodged the fist, pulling his head backwards. 'You're not at your best, Jordan,' he informed her. 'Don't do it. I really don't want to hurt you. It would be a crime to damage that perfect body.'

Undaunted, Jordan took a small hesitant step towards him and raised her hands to his throat. With a grimace, she started the process of tightening her grip, forcing her fingers to constrict his windpipe. I watched Arnold's face distort revealing his discomfort. Very slowly, as Jordan continued, he drew back his sword. His gun was pointed directly at me and John was no longer in any condition to jump him. I could only watch in horror.

'Jordan!' I cried as I saw Arnold's eyes move down Jordan's stomach. She didn't stop as he very deliberately selected his position, resting the tip of the blade against her shirt. Arnold looked at me as his hand twitched, sending the blade into the desired location. It wasn't a deep blow, not designed to kill. I watched him withdraw the tip of the blade. Only two inches of steel had been discoloured by her blood. It was a very precise strike.

Jordan took a sudden breath. Still clutching her hands to his neck, her legs gave way and she fell to her knees. Her head rested against his stomach as she gasped for breath, before she collapsed to the floor, a pool of blood spreading from her wound. I watched in horror as Jordan's laboured breathing continued as she lay still. At least she was alive.

'That was so unnecessary!' Arnold remarked before turning his attention to John. 'Put your head up!' he shouted impatiently, and rested the blade on John's neck again.

'Dance,' he instructed me. 'We don't have much time.'

'No,' I responded with a conviction I didn't feel.

'Dance the dance of Salome,' he demanded in a singsong voice.

'No. My name's not Salome.'

'Dance!' he insisted more forcefully, lowering the sword until it was biting into John's neck.

'No.'

'Dance, or I'll kill him.'

'No,' I repeated, shaking my head. It wasn't much of a choice. 'You'll kill him if I dance.'

'Ah! Very perceptive, little one. If you dance, I'll kill him.

You're quite right.' He looked up at me with a broad smile. 'But if you don't dance, I'll kill them both.' He pointed the gun in his left hand in Jordan's direction and fired a round that made the grass beside her head twitch.

My eyes flicked towards Jordan who had stopped groaning and lay very still. The pool of blood was growing in size and showed no sign of stopping. 'She's already dead,' I pointed out.

Arnold sighed impatiently. 'I can assure you she's alive. The wound isn't deep, but she's losing a lot of blood. Unless you get her to a hospital soon, she will die.'

'How am I supposed to get her to a hospital?'

'The police are already on their way, but I suggest you phone for an ambulance. There's a mobile phone on the bonnet of the car in the barn. They may take some time, but she will survive. She has the constitution of an ox, but you ought to try to stem that bleeding.'

'I'll go and phone.'

As I turned my back, I heard a muted scream: John. When I turned back, the sword had further broken his skin and blood was trickling down both sides of his neck. 'Dance!' he shouted.

I didn't know what to do. Arnold held all the cards. I knew that the moment I started to dance, the sword would strike and John would die. What was the alternative? If I tried to rush him, John might be able to struggle free while he dealt with me. Had Jordan not lost consciousness, she could have distracted him. I was desperately waiting for the sirens of approaching reinforcements.

'I'm waiting!'

If I didn't dance his sick dance, Jordan would die as well,

and I'd incur his anger. There was no guarantee that I'd escape. I didn't want to bargain with a madman, but by dancing, I could possibly save two lives: if he kept his side of the bargain. Tears came to my eyes as I finally realised I couldn't save John. It was his punishment for having been christened with the name of a saint. Maybe Michael would regain his senses long enough to confront Arnold, but I had no idea where he was, or in what condition. Barring a miracle, I could see no way out.

'How do I know you'll let us leave?'

'You have my word. I have my own destiny to fulfil and it doesn't include you. If it had, you'd already be dead. Jordan on the other hand...' He pointed Jordan's gun directly between her eyes to illustrate the point. 'Your friend is getting weaker.'

I looked down. My time for rationalising was over. I'd thought the problem through in the time I'd been allowed. Now my time was up. I cleared my mind and closed my eyes. Tears swept down my cheeks and I could feel my lips quivering. Slowly, my feet began to move. I let out a sob. My soul was in hell. I briefly opened my eyes and saw my feet moving. It was as if they belonged to another woman: they were moving despite my instructions to the contrary. A case of the subconscious taking a decision the conscious mind rejected.

'More!' he urged. 'Faster!'

And I sobbed as I danced, my body joining the rhythm of my feet; my arms moving to the silent beat. It was not a dance Fred Astaire would have recognised and unlike anything that could be seen on the dance floor of a nightclub. The sobbing and heaving of my stomach did nothing to contribute to the consistency of the rhythm, adding uncontrollable twitches to my flailing arms.

'Good!' he said and I watched through tear-stained eyes as he lifted the sword.

'Allison!' cried John as the blade began its descent.

The air was split with a swish as the sword gathered pace. Starting behind Arnold's shoulders, it accelerated, parting the air with a hiss. I watched, stunned into silence as my legs continued their motion. Then there was a hollow thud. John's body twitched furiously. In slow motion, I watched as John's head toppled forward, opening a gaping wound in his neck. Blood pulsed from the exposed neck, staining the ground. His gleaming white vertebrae glittered amidst a scarlet sea. John's kneeling body slowly toppled over onto the grass.

Arnold had done it.

I was petrified: as still as stone and just as cold. I swallowed, unable to take in the full horror of the drama being played out before me. I looked towards Arnold who was wiping the bloodied sword on the grass, leaving long dark smears. My mouth was open and I stared, unable to move. He turned to me and appeared dejected, the sparkle in his eyes gone.

'Go now,' he told me quietly.

I couldn't go. I couldn't move.

'Go!' he shouted. 'And take good care of her,' he added.

The sudden impact of his raised voice shocked me. In a daze, I moved towards Jordan and bent to turn her over and gather her shoulders. Every second I expected to hear the sound of a gunshot or feel the heat of the blade's tip piercing my skin. Behind me, Arnold had plucked John's head from the floor by his hair and placed it on a silver tray. He bent and stared into its open terror-filled eyes. 'Betrayed again,' he mumbled, stroking the hair.

I'd been shocked when I turned Jordan onto her back. Her entire torso was coated with blood, but I could feel a weak heartbeat pumping the remaining blood through her system. With my hands under each shoulder, I hauled her over the ground, an occasional burst of fresh blood issuing from her wound.

I pulled Jordan several yards away, before lying her down carefully. I took off my sweatshirt and bundled it into a ball. Pulling up Jordan's T-shirt, I stuffed the fabric against the wound and applied pressure. I took hold of Jordan's hand and placed it on top of the bundle, helping to keep it in place. Then I stood and ran for the barn. Bursting through the huge wooden door, I saw Michael propped up in a corner. He looked as though he was sleeping peacefully, like a baby. As Arnold told me, the phone was on the car's bonnet. I picked it up and dialled 999. My brain was still functioning rationally enough to inform them that I was a police officer and the situation was an emergency. I summoned police, ambulance and fire brigade, although all three should already have been on their way. I had a feeling I knew how it was going to end.

Then I dialled Inspector Garratt. He was prompt to answer. 'Garratt.'

'It's Allison,' I managed before breaking down.

Garratt could hear the haunted tone and immediately feared the worst. 'Allison! What's happened?' he asked.

Between sobs, I let him have the facts. 'John's dead... Jordan's been stabbed and... Michael's unconscious.'

'Jesus!' he shouted. 'Where's Arnold?'

'He's...' I moved out of the barn towards the house where

I could see the orange hue within the windows. Against the bright blaze, I could see a figure moving towards the front door. 'He's going into the fire. It's burning down.'

'Is anyone else inside?'

I checked the lawn. Jordan still lay where I'd left her, but all that remained of John was his lifeless torso. 'No.'

There was a pause. 'Are you sure Arnold's going inside?'

'Wait!' I took another look, but the scene looked the same, except for the absence of Arnold. The flickering light from the flames made it difficult to be sure. Shadows played around the perimeter. I just couldn't be certain. 'I think that's where he was going. He said he had his 'own destiny to fulfil'.'

'What's that mean?'

'Maybe there's a Saint Lawrence. You'll probably find he burned to death.'

I ended the call as I finally heard sirens approaching. I walked across and bent down beside Jordan. Her eyelids flickered and she drew a shallow breath. I put my hand to her cheek and the eyelids parted marginally. 'You're going to be okay,' I reassured her. Jordan's eyes turned in the direction of the sirens, louder now, coming closer. I tried a smile as I bent down and kissed her gently on her forehead.

I heard the crunch of gravel as the ambulance skidded to a halt. I stood up as the paramedics raced towards me, one dropping beside Jordan. 'Where are you hurt?' I was asked.

'I'm not,' I replied. As I looked down at myself I could understand his concern. My hand and arms and the front of my T-shirt were coated with Jordan's blood. Suddenly, I felt cold and turned to face the building as the first floor windows shattered. I could feel the warmth emanating from the house as it was consumed by fire. Flames licked up the external woodwork and had begun to take hold of the roof. The paramedics quickly loaded Jordan on a stretcher and carried her further away. 'There's another one in the barn. I think he's okay, just drugged.'

One of the medics shook his head as he noticed the headless torso stretched out on the grass. Then he ran to the barn. When he reappeared, Michael was over his shoulder. 'We have to get the girl to hospital,' he said breathlessly. 'What's her name?'

'Jordan,' I replied.

'Jordan what?'

I couldn't remember! Shock was beginning to set in. 'Just Jordan,' I called. 'Take good care of her.'

Chapter 17

I was taken away to hospital, where they checked me over and determined that there was no lasting damage; not physical at any rate. My throat still felt raw from the smoke, but I felt a little better after I was given a dose of pure oxygen. I spent the night there, heavily sedated. When Garratt arrived, I was completely out of it, revelling in the deepest sleep I'd managed since that drug-induced night at the section house. He'd have to wait for his answers. There was no physical reason for me to be in hospital. I just don't think they knew what to do with me.

The following day, I awoke, pretty groggy, around midday. Before I'd even had the chance to get dressed, they were on me: Garratt and Chief Superintendent Jeffries. It was my first meeting with him. I got the impression that Garratt hadn't slept a wink. Presumably, Jeffries had spent the night questioning him about his chosen procedures. Ultimately, the operation had been a disaster and someone had to carry the can. I was pleased that Garratt had waited until he received top-level approval, otherwise he alone would have had to take responsibilty. The only positive crumb of comfort was my belief that Arnold was amongst the casualties.

I suppose my testimony held the key. I didn't think Jordan would have been in any condition to give a statement.

'How do you feel?' asked Garratt gravely.

'I've been better,' I mumbled.

'This is Chief Superintendent Jeffries. He's leading the investigation. He'll want to talk to you later and take a full statement.' He drew a deep breath and took a seat. 'I just wanted to have a chat beforehand to let you know what's been happening. We've managed to keep a lid on things so the press hasn't printed the full story. We're very keen...'

'How's Jordan?' I interrupted.

Garratt considered the question for a moment before responding. 'Jordan's coming along fine. She's in a stable condition but she received some injuries that require specialist treatment. She's been moved to a hospital that specialises in... abdominal injuries. She'll receive the best treatment available.'

'Can I see her?'

Garratt scratched his forehead, looking down seemingly lost for words. Jeffries responded on his behalf. 'Officer Lassiter has requested no visitors,' he stated simply.

I looked at the man, his sombre mask displaying no emotion. His relatively youthful appearance and high rank were evidence enough of his willingness to toe the party line. 'I want to see her.'

'I'm afraid that's not possible.'

I stared at him, a positive dislike growing despite my best efforts to retain my composure. Garratt took up the narrative. 'There are some things you ought to know,' he told me. From a buff folder he extracted a plastic envelope and passed it across the table. 'This was found on Michael's body, tucked into one of the pockets.'

I gazed down at a postcard-sized colour print of a medieval round-faced man with a particularly austere haircut. He wore a purple and gold robe and clutched a bag of money in his left hand. On the rear of the print, a description identified it as a detail from Beato Angelico's St Lawrence Distribut-

ing Alms, which was currently housed in the Vatican. 'How did he die?' I asked, already knowing the answer.

'He was roasted to death on a gridiron.'

I nodded. 'That fits.'

Garratt and Jeffries exchanged a hurried glance, before both averted their eyes.

'What?' I asked.

'Are you sure you saw him entering the burning house?' Jeffries enquired.

I could only shake my head. 'No! He was heading in that direction. Then he was gone.'

Garratt responded with a deep sigh. 'Arnold's body was not found in the remains of the house,' he said grimly.

'What!'

He shook his head. 'Arnold didn't die in the fire.'

'So where the hell is he?'

'We've no idea. We found tyre tracks about two miles from the cottage. We assume they were his.'

'Jesus!' I whispered. When I saw him walking towards the front door, I'd been so sure. He *had* meant to kill himself. The postcard was proof of that. It was to be his ultimate statement and, as he had told me, I was to be his witness.

'Allison!'

'What?' I asked, having heard nothing. I was too stupefied to think straight.

'There's something else,' Garratt told me with a sigh. 'We found this in one of Jordan's pockets when she was at the hospital.' He passed me a familiar clear plastic evidence bag. Inside was another postcard-sized print of a painting.

I picked it up and studied the detail. The figures in the picture gave the impression that they had been taken straight from a medieval court. The women wore sumptuous robes and the men a mixture of armour and ermine-trimmed gowns. A long table occupied the right hand side topped with glasses, a decanter and what looked like several rolls of bread. A figure with a huge beard looked on gravely with his arms folded while a young girl danced in front of him. At the rear, a group of courtiers looked on, while to the left in an enclosed cubicle, a man with a halo and threadbare white gown knelt as a soldier held aloft a sword ready to cut off his head. In a strange transformation of time and space, the young dancing girl was also depicted in the background, kneeling alongside a seated red-robed figure who could have been her mother. The girl was presenting her with a silver tray. Situated on the tray was the man's severed head. I turned the paper over, expecting to see an inscription on the back. There was nothing, but I already knew what the picture depicted and could feel tears welling in my eyes. I felt sick.

'It's by an artist named Benozzo Gozzoli,' explained Garratt. 'It's called 'The Dance of Salome'.'

'John the Baptist,' I muttered.

'Yes. I hadn't realised he was a fully fledged saint, but apparently he is.'

'He was after John all the time,' I remarked sullenly.

'It would appear so.'

'Why?' I muttered.

'What?' Garratt responded.

'Why John?'

He shook his head. 'Why Celia? Why Lucy? We may never know.'

I knew it wasn't as simple as that. There had to be a reason. I just had no idea what it was. His recurrent theme of martyred saints was clearly significant. If we could understand his motivation, maybe we'd be a step closer to finding him.

'Allison!' Garratt said.

I looked up. 'What?' I muttered.

'I was just saying... We'll be maintaining a round-the-clock guard on you and Jordan. In the meantime, every force in the country has been alerted. Arnold's number one on everyone's wanted list.'

'It doesn't matter,' I responded.

'What doesn't matter?' asked Garratt confused.

'He doesn't want me. If he had, he'd have killed me when he had the chance.' I shook my head. 'But Jordan...'

'What about Jordan?' asked Jeffries, suddenly showing an interest.

'When he spoke... It was like he was... in awe of her. I got the impression he knew her.'

'Knew her?' demanded Jeffries.

'But he didn't kill her,' added Garratt unnecessarily. 'He had plenty of opportunity. He must have been very careful when he stabbed her.'

I thought back to the moment when I heard the blade entering Jordan's body: the sickening squelch as it sliced through her flesh. I remembered thinking at the time that it had been a very precise strike. The blade hadn't penetrated far, only the tip was coated with blood as it withdrew. I also had the impression that despite being slowly throttled, he'd glanced down to see exactly where the blade had entered. He'd been aiming for something in particular; something that wouldn't prove fatal. 'He's going after Jordan,' I said simply. 'He said something about protecting her.'

Both men looked up at me with surprise on their faces. Jeffries shook his head. 'We're fairly certain he doesn't want Jordan dead.'

'No, he doesn't want her dead!' I replied. 'He wants her alive.'

'She's being protected.'

'You said they moved her.'

Garratt looked at his watch. 'Yes.'

'Where is she now?'

Garratt shrugged. 'I don't know.'

I sat up, staring at Jeffries. 'Where is she?' I demanded.

'That information is strictly confidential,' he responded. 'The fewer people who know, the better.'

'He's going to get to her!'

'That's not possible. She has a police escort. If you'd just calm down...'

'I need to know where she is.'

Jeffries frowned. Under normal circumstances, I don't believe he would ever have told me her location. Presumably he thought it was safe enough. I was in hospital and wherever I went, it would be with at least one uniformed guard. How much damage could I do?

As he told me the name of the hospital, my blood went cold. I remembered the exaggerated care with which Arnold had selected the position to stab her. He knew exactly which part of her anatomy was going to be injured and he knew where she was likely to end up: at a hospital specialising in gynaecological problems and injuries. When Jeffries told me where she was, I slumped back defeated onto my pillows. It was probably already too late.

Even as I lay in my hospital bed ignoring the protestations of my two visitors, Lawrence Arnold was paying Jordan a visit. She was only just coming round from the effects of the anaesthetic. She was weak and muddled, but would remember enough of their confrontation. Yes, she had a guard stationed outside her door, but there was nothing to stop a fully accredited member of the hospital staff walking straight past; a porter, for instance. If they'd checked his identification badge, they'd have found all his details on their personnel files, right down to a valid National Insurance number. He was that good.

It was the only way to break through the security at St Lawrence's hospital.

The search for Lawrence Arnold
will conclude with *Death & The Angel*.

Lightning Source UK Ltd.
Milton Keynes UK
UKHW040818130920
369834UK00002B/69